ILLUSION ON ICE

BOYS OF WINTER #7

S.R. GREY

Illusion on Ice (Boys of Winter #7)

Copyright © 2019 by S.R. Grey

ISBN-10: 1-7325458-5-5 (print edition)

ISBN-13: 978-1-7325458-5-4 (print edition)

Editing: Hot Tree Editing
Proofreading: Deaton Author Services
Cover Photographer: CJC Photography
Model: Keith Manecke
Cover Design: Najla Qamber

Formatting: E.M. Tippetts

OTHER BOOKS BY
S.R. GREY

Men of Fall series
Forward Progress

Boys of Winter series
Destiny on Ice
Resistance on Ice
Complications on Ice
Caution on Ice
Player on Ice

Judge Me Not series
I Stand Before You
Never Doubt Me
Just Let Me Love You
The After of Us

Inevitability duology
Inevitable Detour
Inevitable Circumstances

Promises series
Tomorrow's Lies
Today's Promises

A Harbour Falls Mystery trilogy
Harbour Falls
Willow Point
Wickingham Way

Laid Bare novella series
Exposed: Laid Bare 1
Unveiled: Laid Bare 2
Spellbound: Laid Bare 3
Sacrifice: Laid Bare 4

A STRANGER IN A STRANGE LAND

MAISIE

I peered out the paned-glass window of the five-star hotel I found myself in—in freaking Stockholm, *Sweden*, no less—and all I could think of was how far from home I was.

You're not in Kansas anymore, Maisie Troy.

No, I sure as hell was not.

Not that I was from Kansas in the first place. Two Palms, a tiny run-down Arizona town near the Nevada state line, was where I laid my head to rest at night.

Or I had until recently.

When I really thought about it, the modest trailer I shared with my former Vegas showgirl mom wasn't much of a home. It hadn't been for a long time, not since my dad left back when I was five.

I sighed, fogging up the paned window.

It just is what it is, Maisie.

That was fine.

I was used to that life, as I'd lived in good ole Two Palms my whole existence. Not that I was old or anything. I was only twenty-one.

I guessed there's a certain amount of comfort in sticking with what you knew.

And in what you're used to.

I leaned forward and pressed my forehead to the cool glass as I thought about my current situation. It sucked, no doubt about that.

So focus on something else.

I did. I peered down ten stories below and watched the vibrant Scandinavian city I was stuck in as it bustled with life.

Those lucky people, I thought.

Swedes were headed off to work, tourists were sightseeing, and construction workers were paving part of the street in front of the hotel.

Everything was as it should be, except for me.

I was a stranger in a strange land, and kind of stranded.

Ah, there was no "kind of" about it.

I was definitely stranded.

Good thing I was making the most of the situation. Not that it was difficult. I liked the city. Stockholm was lively, hip, and urban.

And, wow, was the architecture ever striking, especially over in *Gamla Stan*, or Old Town, located directly across the body of water, Lilla Värtan, just outside my window.

Yeah, it wasn't all bad.

Still, I longed to go home.

Who wanted to stay somewhere where they felt lonely?

Not me.

There was only so much to do in the city all by myself. I didn't have much money on me, so there was a problem already. And, crazy as it sounded, I missed the vast desert outside my modest trailer back at home.

I was nostalgic for the hot dry air that had a habit of creeping in the small window in my bedroom during the day, where it turned crisp and cool at night.

I shouldn't have, but I loved that.

I sighed, as I also missed my dog, Claude. Not that Claude was real. He was a stuffed animal. But he made me feel good and he meant something to me. Probably because he was the only thing my father had ever given to me.

Years ago, before he left.

"Shit," I murmured, my breath fogging the glass once again. "I have to find a way back to the States. I shouldn't even be here, damn it."

I rolled my indigo-blue eyes, big and wide in the reflection, and bit out, "Yeah. Thanks for that, Mom."

Bad enough that I didn't have a dad, but, lucky me, I'd been left in the care of a mom who behaved more like *she* was the child.

I was used to it, though. It'd been that way for as long as I could remember. So, really, it shouldn't have been a big surprise that I was stuck in Stockholm.

Still, I had to be honest with myself. It was partly my fault too, for letting my mom talk me into another one of her misadventures.

She'd begged and pleaded, as was her way, promising we'd have lots of fun.

"Maisie, it'll be the best girl's trip ever," she gushed.

Stupid me, I got caught up in the excitement and believed her. I'd been wearing my rose-colored glasses and didn't even realize it.

That's why I was now paying the price.

Bopping my head against the glass, I chastised, "You're such a fool."

Then I was muttering "ow," because the glass was unforgiving.

No matter, I deserved the pain.

Maybe next time—and there would always be a next time with my mother— I'd pay more attention. I should've known the money was from somewhere suspicious. We weren't the kind of people who had cash lying around for international trips.

"Far from it," I huffed.

Mom sure had played me, telling me she'd won the trip playing slots at a casino across the state line.

How could I have been naïve enough to believe her?

I knew how—I had wanted it to be true, just this once.

But it wasn't.

It was all a lie.

The money had come from a guy.

There's always a guy involved, right?

With my mother there was. And this particular guy was rich. He'd funded the trip. His name was Gary Tarrington, and he owned an international juice company. His signature blend was some kind of lingonberry concoction.

I'd looked it up since then, and had come to learn that lingonberries were pretty big in Sweden.

Just like how Gary was big in Mom's mind.

Worse than the lying, my mother had wasted no time in abandoning me. While I was recovering from jet lag our first night, she was out meeting up with the Juice King.

She called at midnight, waking me.

"Hey, honey, I'm alive and well," she informed me.

"That's good." I checked the clock. "It's 12:00 AM. Where in the hell are you?"

I got a hasty explanation about how she was with Gary and would be for a while.

"Huh, what? What do you mean by 'a while'?"

"Just go back to sleep, Maisie," she'd said, annoyed.

I was too groggy at the time for the gravity of the situation to sink in.

But it sure has sunk in since then.

In six days, Mom has called only once more—to inform me I was on my own.

"It won't be so bad," she'd said. "Enjoy Gary's suite for as long as you like, honey."

I was mad as hell by that point and bit out, "I should've known you didn't win that money playing slots."

"No, no, I didn't," she confessed, chuckling.

Bitch!

"So what happens now, Mom? Our girl's trip is over no sooner than it begun?"

"I'm afraid so, Maisie."

"That's pretty rotten," I mumbled.

She went off then. "Don't start with me, Maisie. You'll be fine; you're an adult. It just is what it is, okay?"

"It's shitty is what it is," I cried out. "You brought me all this way just to leave me stranded and on my own? What was I? Simply a back-up plan in case your guy didn't come through?"

I didn't need a reply. Her bags were gone. I'd definitely been the back-up plan.

"Just tell me this," I said. "Where's the info for my flight home? I'll just call and change the ticket so I can fly back to the States as soon as possible."

"Um, that might be a problem."

A feeling of dread crept up my spine. "Why's that?"

"Well, our tickets may have only been one-way."

"What? May have been, or *were* they only one-way, Mom?"

"They were one way," she confirmed. "But it's okay. Again, just stay in the suite, live the life. You're in a top-notch hotel. Enjoy the perks, Maisie. We don't get chances like this."

I rolled my eyes and muttered, "Oh, yay."

Mom droned on. "Anyway, Gary and I plan to do a little traveling around Europe this summer. Never fear, I'll be in touch at some point."

"You're going to be gone *all* summer?" I yelped, incredulous. "You're kidding, right?"

Mom, nonplussed, replied, "No, I'm not, Maisie."

"What about me?" I whimpered, broken by that point.

"You'll be fine," she reiterated. "You'll probably end up having more fun on your own, anyway."

I choked out a shaky, "How?"

"By going out and meeting people, silly girl."

She was crazy. Hadn't she ever watched the ID channel? I didn't want to become another statistic, damn it!

But she didn't even care.

Drawing in a deep breath, to keep my tears at bay, I said, "Mom, let's get serious here. Me, alone in a foreign city, this is a recipe for disaster."

"No," she countered, "it's a recipe for fun. Don't be such a party pooper."

I tried reasoning with her. "Even in the best case scenario, I'm bound to be discovered. And what happens then? I'll tell you what happens. I get caught and I get thrown out of this hotel. The suite isn't mine, Mom."

She huffed. "You're being silly, Maisie. None of that is a concern. Gary's accountant pays the bill every month, no questions asked. Go ahead, eat and drink like a queen. Do whatever the hell you want, just put it all on the hotel tab and relax."

Though it was a relief to learn expenses weren't a pressing concern, I still wanted out.

So, trying one last time to appeal to my mother's sense of reason, I said, "Look, I don't want to run around the city all by myself. I'd prefer to go home."

Angrily, she hissed, "Sorry, but that just isn't an option right now." *This is weird.*

"Why not?" I asked. "Can't the Juice King just buy me a plane ticket back to the US?"

Mom hemmed and hawed, and finally, in a hushed tone, she said, "Not yet. Okay?"

Uh-oh.

I knew this song and dance.

Warily, I asked, "Mom, what's really going on?"

Something was up, but, not surprisingly, she turned the tables onto me. She was a pro at shit like that.

"Maisie," she began. "Must you always be so difficult and question everything? Just take this as the blessing it is. You're in a country people back home would kill to visit, let alone not have to pay a dime to do so. Go out and enjoy yourself. You're bound to meet a friend you can hang with." Under her breath, she added, "Hopefully it'll be a man. Heaven knows you need one."

Figures, she'd go there.

Grasping at straws, I lamented, "But I don't even speak Swedish."

She had an answer to that one too.

"Practically everyone in Sweden speaks perfect English, honey. You'll get along just fine."

"Mom, please. I just want to go back to Arizona."

Dropping her voice to a hushed whisper, she finally came clean. "Okay, okay, I know. I get it, right? I'll work on that return ticket, I promise. But I can't ask Gary just yet."

"And why is that?" I snapped.

"Because he's not aware I brought you to Sweden, okay?"

"Oh, no." I closed my eyes. "How could that be? If no one knows I'm here, how can I stay in this room? Won't it look suspicious if someone is ordering food and putting crap on a tab?"

Mom snapped back, "I told you no one will be checking, at least not for a while. Gary's accountant doesn't keep constant tabs on his client's whereabouts. He'll simply assume Gary's staying there."

It sounded too simple, and I suspected it wouldn't be that easy to dupe this accountant guy.

I was up shit creek. And I knew I had to do something, something on my own and something drastic, to find my way home.

Putting the crappy call with my mom out of my mind, I went back to blaming myself. Mother had trained me well.

You should've known better and said no to the trip in the first place. Or you could've backed out.

After all, it hadn't been the first time my wanderlust mother had jetted me off so she could meet up with a man.

But, in my defense, the last time had been long ago.

I'd forgotten her MO.

That last time had also only been to LA. Not to somewhere freaking thousands of miles away.

"One thing's for sure," I mused out loud. "You absolutely cannot rely on Mom to help you find your way home."

No, I couldn't count on her to come through.

A fresh round of tears welled in my eyes, blurring the world below.

But as clear as the glass before me, I realized then that, without a doubt, *I* was the only one who could get me out of this mess.

ANOTHER WIN

NOEL

After a hard-fought battle along the boards and behind my team's net, I emerged victoriously with the puck.

Yes!

Skating up ice and over to Team Germany's zone, my forwards remained the perfect distance ahead of me.

I quickly assessed who was most open.

Everyone had been so well-covered throughout the game, making for one hell of an epic defensive battle.

But now we, Team USA, had a chance.

There'd been a defensive breakdown, and my teammate, right winger Blake Cavaletti, was not covered.

So I shot him the puck.

Luckily, it adhered to his stick like there was glue on it.

Cavaletti promptly took off, evading a defenseman who came onto the scene.

Blake played for the New York Rangers back home, and I was with the Las Vegas Wolves. We hadn't known each other for all that long, only since we both arrived in Stockholm to play in these world championships.

We'd clicked right away, though. And Blake had since become my go-to guy on the ice.

Dude was fast as hell, and today was no exception.

After a few more evasive moves, outsmarting three of Team Germany's best players, Blake scored.

I whooped, "Fuck, yeah. That's how you do it, Cavaletti!"

We were now up 2-1. And there were only a couple of minutes left to play.

We transitioned to a tight defensive lockdown mode.

Team Germany never had a chance.

We won the game, advancing us to the semifinals.

Hell yes!

It was exactly what I'd needed after the past month.

I decided to join Team USA after the Wolves were knocked out of the playoffs. I freaking loved hockey, man, and felt like I had a lot left in the tank.

What a great decision.

Ever since I'd arrived in Stockholm, I was playing hockey every day. I also got the pleasure of hanging out with an awesome group of guys.

What could be better than that?

My brain had an answer. Or maybe it was my heart doing the talking, since what I heard was: *If you had someone to share all this with, Noel, it'd be a little more worthwhile, yeah?*

"Ah, shut up," I grumbled, even though I knew my damn heart was right.

My life really was missing something. I felt lonely all the time. I was ready, really ready to share my life with someone.

Ha, like that'll ever happen.

Since we were in the locker room now that the game was over, Blake threw a towel over at me.

"What are you mumbling about over there, Sandlund?" he asked, laughing.

"Ah, it's nothing." I shrugged. "Just reviewing some plays in my head and talking out loud."

Yeah, I wasn't about to share my mushy, woe-is-me thoughts with the whole freaking team. The mood in the room was celebratory, as it should have been, what with our big win and all.

Smoothing back his jet-black hair, wet from showering, Blake said, "That sure was one hell of a game, right? Your battle behind the net was fucking stellar. You were strong on your skates, and it paid off for us."

Not one to revel in my own success, I waved off the praise. "Nah, I was just doing my job as a defenseman."

"Well," Blake replied, "you just keep on doing that, okay?"

I gave him a thumbs-up. "Will do."

More guys joined in the conversation then, and we chatted for a bit about our win There was also some good-natured ribbing on how I wasn't one for hitting up the clubs and bars after the games.

"Let me guess, Sandlund," someone yelled from the back of the locker room. "You're heading straight over to the hotel, like usual."

I ignored whoever the smartass was, but when Blake asked the same thing, I confirmed, "Yeah, I think I will just head back."

"Aw, come on, Noel." Blake shot me a pleading look. "Break from your usual routine just this once and come out with us."

I ran my hand through my messy dark blond hair.

It made me think of how people in Sweden often mistook me for a native Swede. It wasn't just the hair, though. I was also tall and had blue eyes. My grandparents hailed from Sweden, so it made sense.

And that's when a little voice in my head chimed in about how my grandparents would want me to go out and enjoy the city, especially to celebrate my win.

Ah, what the hell.

Blowing out a breath, I said to Blake, "Where are you guys going?"

He looked pleased that I'd asked. "We're just heading out to dinner, man. Nothing crazy."

Hmm…

Most nights the boys went out clubbing after games. I wasn't opposed to partying and having a good time, but at twenty-five, I was beginning to feel as if I'd been there, done that. I also really wanted to stay focused on hockey.

But since it was just dinner, I nodded and said, "Okay, count me in."

3

A NECESSARY PLAN

MAISIE

After spending the day holed up in my hotel room, I finally broke down and ordered room service for a late dinner.

Not only was I famished—I hadn't eaten since the day before—but I felt like I should gather some intel so I could formulate a plan to get back to the US.

Nothing had changed; I wasn't about to rely on my mom.

Lucky for me, the teenage kid who delivered the food was not immune to my feminine wiles.

One bat of my long dark lashes and a strategic flip of my shiny black hair, and the kid was putty in my hands.

When I asked him if there was anyone interesting staying in the hotel, he immediately replied, "Team USA has the whole second floor."

"Team USA?" I cocked my head. "Do you mean the hockey team?"

There'd been a lot of coverage lately about some sort of a hockey championship being played in town.

"I sure do," the kid confirmed.

Hmm, I could possibly work with this.

An all-male hockey team on the premises meant there'd be many guys to choose from—all young and around my age, most of them from NHL teams. I knew they'd all had lots and lots of money.

It was perfect.

Plus, bonus, every single one of them was from the good ole US of A.

Well, there were Canadians in the mix too. But that was close enough. At least we'd be talking the same continent.

All of those players would have to go home at some point after the championship games ended. Maybe I'd have a chance to get to know at least one of them well enough to convince him to buy me a ticket back to the States.

That's it!

I absolutely had to do this—I had to make my own chance and get one of these hockey guys interested in me.

It shouldn't be that hard. I was my mother's daughter, after all. And I had my ways.

Coyly, I asked the kid what Team USA's schedule looked like this week.

After a moment of thought, he replied, "I'm not sure. But I do know they played a game earlier today."

"Oh, they did, did they?"

The wheels were a-turning.

"Yes, miss," he said.

"Do you know if the players usually come straight back to the hotel after the games?"

If that were the case, I'd probably have to skip dinner. It would've been a shame, as I'd ordered a big juicy steak, salad, and boiled potatoes, putting it all on Gary's handy tab, of course.

Thanks, Juice King.

Ugh, but the thought of the man who had caused my predicament made me feel ill. So much so that I felt compelled to give the side of lingonberries that had come with my dinner a dirty look.

The kid didn't notice, thank God. He was too busy explaining how the Team USA guys usually went out after the games and arrived to the hotel much later.

"Like what time?" I asked.

"Around eleven or midnight," he said.

Excellent.

I turned to check the clock by the bedside table. It was only a little after eight. I'd have plenty of time to eat and get ready.

I definitely wanted to spend more time on the "getting ready" part. I'd need to look my best to land a hot hockey dude.

Before the kid left, I gave him a huge tip on the receipt I had to sign.

He thanked me, and I told him, "Not a problem."

I chuckled.

Hey, the Juice King could afford it.

Once I was all alone, I pulled the cart over to my king-sized bed and sat down on the edge so I could eat my dinner. There was a side room with a dining table and chairs, but eating in that room felt too formal.

"Maybe if I had someone to dine with," I lamented.

But I didn't, so this was it.

It wasn't so bad. Everything was delicious, leading me to conclude that I'd have to treat myself more often.

On the Juice King's dime, of course.

Prior to that evening, I'd been grabbing the free breakfast down at the hotel's morning buffet, and then purchasing open-faced sandwiches from street vendors for lunch or dinner. I'd been using the little bit of cash I had converted to Swedish Krona.

Shrimp and cucumbers on dark rye bread were super yummy, I'd discovered. But they couldn't compare to a real meal like the one I was devouring.

Once I was done, I felt satiated and ready to play my role.

I rolled the room service cart out into the hall and headed off to the bathroom, where I slipped out of my sweats and tee and settled into a luxurious bubble bath.

One thing for sure, the suite certainly was decadent.

In the big claw-footed tub, I began to formulate my plan, my necessary plan.

I'd head down to the hotel bar in about an hour. Once I was there, I'd secure a spot where any incoming players could clearly see me. Hopefully, a few of them would show up. It seemed likely, seeing as they all went out drinking after the games, or so the kid had said.

Someone always wanted the party to continue, right?

I sure as hell hoped so.

My next consideration was what to wear.

I had to garner the attention of a young, hot hockey player, so I'd need to look pretty damn good myself.

That meant something sexy was in order.

How fortuitous that I'd packed a slinky black dress.

Ah, men were so easy.

I smiled as I popped a bubble in the tub.

Yep, if all went according to plan, I'd have that ticket home in no time.

4

WHO'S THAT GIRL?

NOEL

Dinner with the guys turned out to be a lot more fun than I expected. I was glad I had tagged along. Still, when they announced that they were headed to some hip club, I opted to return to the hotel.

It was weird.

I'd just been in a real funk lately.

It wasn't simply about getting older and not wanting to party. I just felt like something was missing in my life.

As I walked back to the hotel along the streets of Stockholm, I glanced around.

It was summertime and still daylight out, so the streets were full.

As I took an assessing glance this way and that, the people who stood out to me the most were the couples.

There were a lot of them, probably because it was Friday, a customary date night.

When an elderly pair holding hands strolled by me, something tugged in my chest.

It was my heart, longing for something more. I was done denying the truth. What that older couple had was what *I* wanted.

Once upon a time, I hadn't cared one way or the other about relationships. Sure, I'd dated my share of women, many of whom were smart and beautiful, but I was always too busy with hockey to take things to the next level.

Truthfully, I hadn't had the will or inclination to work on building a real relationship.

But I freaking wanted one now.

That was probably why, when I walked into the hotel lobby and saw the most stunningly beautiful girl heading into the bar, I followed her.

Who's that girl?

Fuck, I had to find out.

I didn't want to come off like a creeper, though. So when she sat down on one side of the long L-shaped oak bar, crossing her long, lithe legs in the process, I smoothly detoured to the short end.

It was perfect; I still had a great view of her.

And fuck, what a sight she was.

The captivating girl had the shiniest long raven hair I'd ever seen, flowing enticingly down her back. She had a really pretty face too. And her body, fuck, I wanted to do sinful things to every inch of it.

She was slender but curvy in all the right places, and rocking a dress made of some sort of clingy black crepe material. The dress had long sleeves and a high neck, but was super short.

Suffice it to say, it was sexy.

And so was she.

I ordered a vodka tonic when the bartender came around, thinking *to hell with abstaining.*

I needed a drink to settle my ass.

This woman excited me, and my male hormones were firing on all cylinders, urging me to get up and go over and talk with her.

I wanted to play it cool, though.

At least, initially.

There was always a chance she was meeting someone.

Yeah, that'd be real fucking smooth, Noel. Making a move on her just as her date walks in.

Talk about awkward.

So, yeah, no, there was no rush. I could bide my time.

I was glad I still had on the dark suit I'd worn to dinner. I wouldn't have wanted to look like a bum.

I nursed my drink after it arrived, chuckling when I noticed how the bartender was taking every opportunity to talk to the stunning girl. Even when she had a full glass of wine in front of her, he checked in on her every other minute. The guy was clearly captivated by the gorgeous woman.

Who could blame him?

So was I.

I was sneaking in glances every chance I could.

Although I was pretty sly about it, so it didn't matter. It helped that the bartender was keeping her preoccupied with his oh-so-blatant flirting.

The girl was smiling and engaging in conversation with him, but it seemed hollow. I sensed she wasn't really into him.

Good.

Suddenly, my phone dinged.

I checked and saw it was Blake.

He wanted to know if I was interested in rejoining the boys. They were at a bar just down the road.

Was he kidding? I had better things to do.

Another time, I texted back.

Dude, you are so boring.

I laughed.

I didn't feel "boring" at the moment. I knew any one of those fools would've loved to have been hanging at *this* bar, seated close to an absolutely stunning woman. It had to beat whatever the hell it was they were doing.

When I looked up from my phone, I noticed the girl was eyeing me curiously.

Interesting…

I'd been so worried about her busting me.

Maybe she wouldn't have minded?

Hell, she was not only peering over at me, but was that a smile I detected?

Yes, yes it was.

The beautiful girl I'd followed in, in the hopes of having a chance to talk to, was definitely smiling over at me.

If that isn't an invitation, I don't know what is.

5

I FIND MY MARK

MAISIE

Oh, crap, the guy I was smiling at is getting up and coming over to me. Eek!

The gorgeous blond dude who was seated at the short end of the bar, sneaking in surreptitious glances my way, was definitely heading my way.

Help!

I wanted to get his attention, but now that I had it, I kind of panicked.

I had a plan, but implementing it wouldn't be easy. I hated the idea of purposely misleading someone. I wasn't that kind of sneaky bitch.

Maisie, get it together. You can't mess this up.

This guy was my ticket home. And now he was my "mark."

I decided as much after the friendly bartender informed me that my admirer from down the bar was one of the hockey players from Team USA. He also mentioned that the guy played for an NHL team, but he wasn't sure which one.

When I pressed him, he said he thought it might be the Wolves. Since I wasn't a big hockey fan, I had no idea which city that team was from.

Looked like I was about to find out.

I couldn't believe things were set into motion so soon. It was like fate was on my side.

As the hockey dude approached, cool as could be, I rolled back my shoulders.

Yes, I could do this.

Not that I had much of a choice.

Money wasn't going to up and appear out of nowhere. And I needed that damn plane ticket home. Mom was unreliable, and I had no desire to stick around in Stockholm all summer.

Ha, that was the best-case scenario.

If the accountant who monitored Juice King's hotel activity discovered he wasn't really staying in his suite, I'd be thrown out on my ass. Then I'd be homeless on the streets of a country where I didn't even speak a lick of their language.

Shit, I have to get out of here.

Hockey dude was my best chance.

How bad could it be, anyway?

The guy was beyond hot, sexy too.

I saw that when he sauntered up and murmured a low and husky, "Hey."

Ooh, his voice was smokin'. And those sparkling blue eyes were nothing short of captivating.

I could peer into them all day.

I was about to too.

But no!

I had to get my shit together, reclaim the upper hand.

Flipping back my wavy tresses, I threw out a nonchalant, "Hey back at you."

His cool façade faltered.

Good, I wanted to disarm him. It would make him more pliable.

He cleared his throat, no doubt pulling his shit together like I'd been doing, and then said, "I noticed you were over here all alone."

Okay, so he wasn't exactly Mr. Smooth. It was cute, though. I knew I could work that to my advantage.

"Yes," I replied coolly, "you noticed correctly."

Gesturing to the empty bar stool next to me, he asked, "Is it okay if I join you?"

I shrugged, maintaining my devil-may-care attitude. "Sure. Knock yourself out."

Smiling a pearly white grin, he sat down and remarked, "You sound American."

"I am," I confirmed, adding a bit more friendliness to my tone.

Couldn't be too much of a bitch and scare him off. I wanted this man to like me, right?

"So," he said, relaxing as I hoped he would. "Where are you from in the States?"

"Arizona," I replied. "And since you're obviously American too, where are you from?"

"Nevada. Las Vegas, to be exact."

"No way!" Caught off guard, I blurted out, "We're practically neighbors."

This was great. If I returned to the US with him, we'd surely fly into Las Vegas. And my town was just over the state line.

It couldn't get much better than this.

"So," I began, turning my own dazzling smile hockey dude's way. "Do you have a name, guy from Nevada?"

He laughed. "Yes, girl from Arizona, I do. My name is Noel, Noel Sandlund." He reached out to shake my hand. "And you are?"

I took his hand, and, whoa, *fireworks!*

His hand was so freaking warm, his grasp firm and manly. I wondered what he could do to me with those fingers I was touching.

Oh, my.

Not thinking straight at all, I blathered, "Nice to meet you, Noel. I'm Maisie. Maisie Troy."

Oops.

Yanking my hand away, I swallowed hard.

Fuck.

I had just divulged my last name to my mark.

How stupid was that?

I'd been planning to make up a fake one.

Okay, so I clearly sucked at this covert game. My only hope now was that he'd forget it.

"Maisie?" Noel looked at me with concern, his brow creasing. "You look super upset all of a sudden. Is everything okay?"

I waved my hand in the air, quickly schooling my features to calm and happy.

"No, everything is fine. It's just, I, uh…"—*think of something, fast!*—"…my stomach felt a little weird there for a minute. I ordered room service earlier, and I don't know, maybe Swedish food just doesn't agree with me."

What a lame excuse, Maisie. You didn't have anything Swedish to eat. Not to mention, you actually love their cuisine.

Making matters worse, Noel proceeded to ask, "Really? What did you have?"

I'd had steak, but I couldn't exactly tell him that. Not a Swedish-centric dish in the slightest.

So I fibbed, "Uh, I had Swedish meatballs."

He nodded, commiserating. "I hear ya. The rich gravy that comes on those things can be a bit much."

Aw, he was sweet.

But wait, why does he have to be so nice?

It's going to suck taking advantage of him.

I dismissed all that, as I couldn't exactly entertain guilt and get this shit done.

So, nodding, I said, "Yeah, for sure."

Ugh, my stomach really was starting to hurt. And it wasn't because of any food.

No, the prospect of duping someone, especially a clearly nice guy like Noel, was not exactly pleasant.

But I was backed into a corner. I was trapped.

What choice did I have?

6

I LIKE MAISIE. I LIKE HER A LOT

NOEL

One thing was for sure—Maisie Troy was an interesting woman. Not only was she more beautiful up close, she seemed sweet and nice. She'd been a bit standoffish at first, but she was loosening up.

How cool was it that she was from the States?

Arizona, we really were practically neighbors.

If something developed between us, we could keep on seeing each other back home.

Yeah, there was definite potential here.

Wouldn't it be crazy if I'd had to come all this way to meet the woman I was searching for all along?

Shit, wait. I was getting *waaay* ahead of myself.

I didn't even know this chick.

But I *wanted* to know her.

So I asked her, "What brings you to Sweden, Maisie Troy?"

She winced when I said her last name.

Okay, that's weird.

Was she hiding something?

No, that can't be right.

She didn't look dangerous at all, except maybe to my heart.

Fiddling with the stem of her wineglass—and making an effort to not look at me at all—she said, "I flew over here with, uh, a friend for vacation. But she met a guy and left with him."

Whoa, I didn't expect that.

"Jesus," I gasped. "So you're here all alone?"

"Yep, I am."

"Well that totally sucks."

"Tell me about it."

"Yeah, wow."

Maisie finally met my gaze, but she was smiling sadly. "Hey, at least I have a really cool room all to myself. It's a suite too, so there's that."

I wanted to make her feel better, so I replied with an enthusiastic, "Nice!"

"Yeah," she muttered. "I guess."

I was curious about something, though, prompting me to ask, "Do you plan on sticking around Stockholm for a while? Or are you thinking about heading back to Arizona right away?"

Again, she glanced away. "Um, I don't know. I guess I'm sort of playing it by ear at the moment."

Okay, that made sense.

"Taking it day by day, huh?" I nodded approvingly.

"Yeah, something like that."

Maisie was a little quirky, sure, but I liked her.

Finishing off her wine, she set the glass down and said, "Enough about me. Tell me why you're in Sweden, Noel."

I pointed up to a TV that just happened to be replaying our earlier hockey match-up. "I'm a hockey player. I played in that game earlier today."

"What? No way!" Blinking up at the screen, but not seeming as surprised as I'd expected she'd be, she said, "That's cool. So you're on Team USA?"

I smiled proudly as I replied, "I sure am."

"So I'm sitting with a real live hockey player." She took me in and nodded. "Wow, color me impressed."

She was saying all the right things, but something was off. For all her bluster, I sensed she'd already known I was a hockey player.

That prompted me to ask, "Do you follow hockey pretty closely, Maisie?"

"No, not at all." She shook her head. "I do know some of the NHL team names, but not where they're from. Do you play for one of those?"

"I do," I replied. "I'm with the Las Vegas Wolves."

She smacked her head. "That's right. You just said that you lived in Las Vegas. I should've put two and two together."

Again, it was like she *had* known and was just playing it off.

No, I was being paranoid. It'd been so long since I'd chatted up a beautiful woman that I was losing my touch.

Yeah, man, get it together.

Since her wineglass was empty, I asked her if she'd like another.

"Sure, thanks. That'd be great," she replied.

When the bartender came around, shooting daggers at me the whole time, I ordered us another round.

As he was walking away, I leaned into Maisie and said, "I think he likes you."

"Nah," she murmured softly.

She was definitely underestimating her attractiveness. And that made me like her even more.

Yeah, I liked Maisie. I liked her a lot.

So I took a chance and decided to ask her out.

Clearing my throat, I said, "Since we're both in town for who knows how long, would you like to do something sometime?"

Glancing up at me through her long dark lashes—*kill me now*—she coyly replied, "Are you asking me out on a date, Noel from Nevada?"

I arched a brow. "If I were, Maisie from Arizona, would you say yes?"

"Hmm," she said, smiling, "I think I might."

Ah, I liked this woman.

She was charming and fun.

"Then yes," I stated, puffing out my chest. "I'm asking you out on a date."

Laughing, she accepted, and we made arrangements to go to dinner the very next night.

7

CHARMED

MAISIE

My date with Noel was swiftly approaching, and I still had no idea what to wear.

I knew dinner was on the menu, no pun intended, but he'd mentioned when we texted that he had "something special" planned for afterward.

With no idea what that could mean, I didn't know how to dress.

Standing in the middle of my hotel bedroom, with nothing on but a silky black bra and matching panties, I declared, "Fuck it. I'm going all out."

Marching over to the big walk-in closet, I grabbed a silver sequin minidress off a hanger.

"So long as we're not going ice skating or anything crazy like that, I should be good," I stated.

After I slipped the dress over my head, I stepped into a pair of sleek black pumps.

Ah, I was ready.

Cool. It's close to seven. Noel should be here any minute.

I figured there was no harm in giving him my room number. He was bound to end up here anyway, especially if things progressed. Plus, it was kind of sweet that he wanted to officially pick me up for our date.

I sighed.

There was something about Noel that made him stand out as an amazing guy, something more than his tall stature, his achingly handsome face, and his mega-muscular body.

I actually liked *him*, or at least I liked the person he seemed to be. He was easy to talk with. And he was nice.

Nice was good. I'd had enough jerks in my past.

Two Palms, unfortunately, seemed to have a dearth of gentlemen.

But what was I?

I was kind of being a jerk to Noel by misleading him.

"Damn it," I bit out.

I thought about just coming clean and filling Noel in on the truth—that I was stuck here in Sweden and needed help.

The only problem was I had no idea how he might react.

Sure, he *seemed* like a nice guy.

But I didn't really know.

Noel might turn out to be cool and lend me the money I needed for a plane ticket home, not that I could ever hope to repay him in any kind of timely manner. But there was also the possibility he could tell me to get lost.

No, I couldn't take that chance. I had to continue to pretend I was a carefree girl staying in Stockholm, playing it by ear.

Back to cultivating that exact illusion, I stepped out of the closet and back into the bedroom, debating on whether to wear my long hair up or down.

Just as I peered into the mirror above the dresser and decided on down, someone knocked.

I stared at my reflection. "Shit, he's here."

Fluffing out my raven locks to maximum sexy volume, I hurried back out to the main room of the suite and flung open the door.

Wow!

Noel was smokin'.

We just kind of nodded to each other, both of us dazzled. I knew I sure was.

"Hey," I said at last.

"Hi."

We stood there, taking each other in a minute longer. I didn't know what he was thinking, but I freaking loved the way he looked tonight. The black dress pants, shiny black shoes, and crisp white button-down he had on made him look like he'd just stepped from the pages of *GQ*.

I swallowed hard.

Hockey players have the best bodies, I swear.

It was abundantly clear from the way Noel's clothes fit him that he was in phenomenal shape. That made me wonder just how good he looked *out* of those clothes.

I'd have to find out.

"Mmm, yes," I murmured, licking my lips.

Noel caught that and let out a light chuckle.

You are so busted.

"Uh…" I leaned to my right, fumbling for my clutch on the table by the door, and hoping to also find my dignity there.

I don't know if I found that, but I did locate the clutch.

"I'm ready," I said, straightening.

"Okay, cool."

Suddenly nervous, I began to ramble.

"Are you ready? Of course you're ready. You're at my door, right?"

Someone stop me!

Noel didn't seem to mind my blathering. In fact, I think he liked it.

Oh, what the hell.

I decided to own up to having just been caught ogling him.

"Quit smiling so smugly," I chastised as I stepped out into the hall to join him, the door closing behind me with a click. "You *know* you look good."

Appearing both pleased and surprised at the same time, he said, "Why thank you, Maisie. But let's be honest, I can't hold a candle to you. You, m'lady, are one truly stunning woman."

He was serious, but I felt compelled to dial it down a notch. We shouldn't lay all our cards on the table just yet, right?

Fluttering my lashes, I teased, "My, aren't you the little charmer, Noel from Nevada?"

He leaned in close, and God, he smelled amazing.

While I was busy breathing him in, hopefully in a way he wouldn't notice, he murmured seductively, "Just wait till you see our transportation for the night. Hopefully you'll continue to feel *charmed*."

So much for dialing it back a notch. We were clearly too damn attracted to one another to play nonchalant.

I decided to just roll with it, let the flirtation flow.

Bumping his hip with mine, I said just as seductively, "So show me, Noel. I can't wait to see everything you have planned for me tonight."

He raised a brow. "Is that so?"

"You bet your ass it is."

"Good." Chuckling, he gallantly offered his arm. "Shall we head down to the lobby, then?"

What a gentleman.

"Yes."

I slid my arm in his and we headed over to the elevator, where Noel pressed the Down button.

Once we were in the lobby, I saw right away that there was a sleek black limo parked outside the hotel entrance. I knew that was the "transportation" he'd alluded to.

Leaning in to Noel as we walked toward the revolving glass entryway, I murmured, "And so the charming continues, I see."

"Ahh, you're so onto my devious plan."

I swallowed hard. Little did he know I was the one with the devious plan.

But there was no time for guilt.

Clearing my throat, I said, "Pulling out *all* the stops for our first date. I like it."

"Good, you deserve nothing but the best, Maisie from Arizona."

Oh, if only that were true.

Once we were outside the hotel, the driver jumped from the limo to open my door.

Noel beat him to it, though.

As I slid into the long back seat, he and I smiled at each other. I could've gazed into his beautiful blues forever, but we needed to get going.

Noel closed the door, went to the other side, and slipped in next to me.

I couldn't help but murmur, "Alone at last."

He nodded up to the driver. "Well, almost."

"Mmm, yes."

I crossed my legs strategically, and just as I planned, my dress rode up, exposing quite a bit of bare thigh.

Yes, it was my turn to throw a little of my own charm Noel's way.

It worked too

His gaze dropped to my legs, where he unapologetically lingered.

When I asked him a random question about how far away the restaurant was, he couldn't even answer.

"Huh, what?" he said.

Score one for me.

"Ahem." I cleared my throat, trying like hell not to laugh at this turn of events. "I'm up here, Mr. Sandlund."

He glanced up, but his expression held no remorse for having just been caught ogling me.

In fact, he flat-out stated, "You are beyond beautiful, Maisie."

That took me aback. "Uh, um, thanks?"

My heart skipped a beat, and I didn't know what else to say. Noel's words had hit me hard because he'd uttered them with such raw honesty and conviction.

I'd very much gotten to him.

I should've been thrilled.

But I genuinely liked him. And that made the victory bittersweet.

Noel would eventually find out I was an illusion, and he'd hate me forever.

I COULD GIVE HER STOCKHOLM

NOEL

wanted so badly to sweep Maisie off her feet. For some reason it was important to me. I needed this night, our first date, to be special.

There were so many good things about her. Like, as attractive as she was, she didn't give off any conceited or entitled vibes. I liked that. And Maisie was really open and honest. It was great how she'd had no qualms about letting me know she found me attractive. Her ogling me at the hotel had taken me aback, but in a totally good way.

And now that we were on our way to the restaurant, I couldn't keep my damn eyes off her.

Of course it didn't help that she was wearing such a short and sexy dress. It seemed no matter which way she turned, I was afforded another delicious view of her shapely, toned legs.

That led to me imagining just how those legs would look wrapped around me.

Better yet, how would they *feel* wrapped around me?

"Damn." I swiped at my brow.

"What's wrong, Noel?" Maisie asked.

"Nothing." I shook my head. "Just, does it feel hot in here to you? I'm freaking burning up."

Looking rather smug—clever girl—she told me the limo felt just fine to her.

She was probably right.

Still, I pressed the button to lower the tinted window a crack.

As some much-needed cool night air rushed in, I murmured, "Ah, that's much better."

It wasn't better for long, though. With the window down, Maisie caught sight of where we were headed and leaned her lithe body across my lap to garner a better view.

"Oooh, did we just drive into Old Town?" she asked excitedly as she lowered the window some more. "I see it from my room all the time, but I've never walked over."

Huh, that was curious.

"Why haven't you gone over?" I asked.

Maisie twisted toward me, and I had to press my back into the leather seat so her boobs weren't smashed up against my chest. Not that I would've minded, but I was trying to remain a gentleman.

Still, a man can only take so much.

I let out a pent-up breath, and Maisie realized just how close we were.

Quietly sliding back to her own side, she murmured, "Sorry."

But it was like she was anything but.

I muttered back a raspy, "Hey, I'm not complaining."

Quickly, she returned to talk of Old Town, probably because it felt safer for her.

Definitely a safer subject for me, seeing as I couldn't stop thinking about what it'd be like to kiss Maisie, and have her body pressed close to mine once more.

Cool it, Noel.

You're going to show your hand too soon and scare her off.

I calmed down a bit, catching up to Maisie just as she was saying, "Yeah, I've really wanted to come over to Old Town. I just didn't want to do it alone."

I smiled over at her. "Well, you're here now. And you're not alone."

Her pretty eyes, which I noticed were the most unique shade of blue-violet, met mine.

"Yeah, you're right," she said softly. "I'm not alone. Thanks for that, Noel."

I took a chance and reached for her hand.

She didn't resist, and we ended up holding hands till we reached the restaurant.

The place I'd chosen was in the heart of Old Town, located on a cobblestone side alley, tucked between a gift shop and a florist.

This particular restaurant was one of the oldest in Stockholm. And Maisie and I were about to have a private dinner by candlelight down in the cozy stone cellar.

We walked in, and the hostess came up to us. She took my name, and led us over to a set of narrow, roughly hewn steps going down to the cellar.

Cautiously, we made our way down behind her. I kept my hand at the small of Maisie's back to steady her, seeing as she had on high heels.

Once we reached the base of the stairs, the hostess ushered us into a small stone alcove adjoined to the cellar.

It was a tight space, and I had to lower my head to make it through the entryway.

Even though we were in the basement of the restaurant, there was no hint of cold or dampness. The small space was actually warm and cozy, alit by dozens of candles.

"Here's where you'll be dining," the hostess announced, gesturing to a small wooden table in the center of the room.

"Excellent," I said. "Thank you."

As soon as she left, Maisie exclaimed, "Noel, this is so romantic."

She spun around in a circle, her sequin dress sparkling in the glow of the candles.

Laughing, I replied, "I'm glad you like it."

"Like it? Are you kidding? I love it."

I was pleased with Maisie's reaction. It was exactly the response I'd been hoping for.

Once we were seated at our table, we smiled at one another. A waiter then appeared with a bottle of wine. And since glasses were already on the table, he filled each one quite generously.

"Should we toast to anything?" Maisie asked once we were once again alone.

I raised my glass. "Yes. How about we toast to promising starts?"

"Mmm..." Her eyes sparkled in the candlelight. "I like that one."

Our glasses touched, echoing a little *clink*. And together, we said, "To promising starts."

A few minutes later, as we were sipping our wine, the waiter returned with menus.

We made our selections soon afterward—salad, salmon, and

steamed potatoes.

He told us we'd made excellent choices, and then slipped away, leaving us alone once more.

I asked Maisie to tell me more about her life, but she aptly turned the questioning back to me.

"Oh, I'm boring," she pshawed. "I want to hear more about you and hockey."

Since I was always up for talking about the sport I loved, I said, "Okay. What do you want to know?"

"Well, you're a defenseman, right?"

Cocking a brow, I replied, "Hmm, sounds like someone's been googling me."

She blushed, which was so damn adorable.

"Okay, okay. I may have looked you up once or twice."

"A woman who does her research," I replied. "I like it."

She laughed. "Okay. Well, based on that research, I thought of a question."

"Shoot."

"How do you like playing your position? I read that you're fairly offensive minded. Do you sometimes wish you were a forward?"

Wow, she really had done her research.

Thoroughly impressed, I explained that, though I liked to score, I enjoyed my job as a defenseman far too much to want it any other way.

"Besides," I went on, "it's good defense that ultimately wins the game."

Maisie pondered that, and then said, "That makes sense."

I nodded. "For me, that's really the bottom line. When I do my job well, it gives our team a chance to score goals and win."

"You like winning, Noel. Don't you?" Maisie asked.

"Yes, I do."

When she didn't say anything more, I asked, "Don't you?"

She shrugged. "I don't know. I guess you could say I haven't had much luck in the winning department."

I was confused. I wanted to ask for more elaboration, but the salads arrived just then.

Figures.

As we ate our leafy greens, the conversation turned light, and continued so with the arrival of our entrees.

Maisie, after taking her first bite of salmon, announced, "Mmmm, this is so good, Noel."

I tasted mine and had to agree, "It is."

As dinner progressed, I grew more and more excited. I was really looking forward to the next part of our date. I couldn't wait to see Maisie's reaction.

I couldn't believe I'd managed to secure the rooftop of our hotel, where the view of Stockholm was phenomenal. It was such an ideal summer night for sitting outside too. I knew we'd have a great time.

Maisie thought she liked Old Town?

Ha, I couldn't wait for her to find herself twelve stories above it, seated in a big wooden Adirondack chair, the whole city at her feet.

I may not have been able to give Maisie the world, but I could give her Stockholm.

9

CANDLELIGHT AND TEARS

MAISIE

Noel was sweeping me off my feet, treating me better than any man had ever treated me.

I wasn't used to guys like him. Back in my little Podunk town, there wasn't a great selection of men, and the few I had dated had all been pretty much jerks.

Oh, but I could get used to this.

I enjoyed the romantic candlelit dinner, but now that we were back at our hotel, seated up on the rooftop, I was in awe.

We were high above Stockholm, in side-by-side long wooden lounge chairs, sipping wine as darkness fell.

The lights of the surrounding buildings flickered to life, and I sighed contentedly.

I finally felt at peace for the first time since I'd arrived in the city.

And it was all because of Noel.

He looked over at me, his blue eyes pale in the low light.

His gaze was curious as he asked, "Are you having a nice evening, Maisie?"

"Yes, it's amazing," I replied truthfully. "And I'm thoroughly impressed you were able to not only rent out the restaurant cellar, but this entire rooftop as well."

He shrugged. "Oh, it was nothing."

"Oh, but it is indeed something," I volleyed back.

This man had done all this for me, and it was only our first date.

Wow.

If Noel put this much effort and care into one night, I could only imagine what he might do for a woman he truly cared for.

I didn't want to think about that, though. We'd never be more because I hadn't been truthful. A real relationship could never be built on falsehoods.

Did it even matter?

I reminded myself that this was nothing more than a means to an end. Even if I wanted to continue something with Noel once we returned to the States, a guy like him would never want a girl like me. I lived in a freaking trailer, for fuck's sake.

Meanwhile, he rented out rooftops and private rooms in restaurants like it was nothing.

Our worlds were just far too different.

But for now, I could be what he wanted.

I had to be, right?

Reaching over, I took his hand in mine.

"You may think all this is nothing, Noel," I reiterated, "but trust me, it's definitely something."

Adjusting so that my hand was in his, he squeezed lightly and replied, "I just wanted this night to be special for you…and for us."

"Well, it is." I let go of his hand so I could move our chairs a little closer. "It most definitely is."

"So…" He smiled over at me. "Tell me more about you, Maisie from Arizona. You're not getting off so easily this time. You deflected well at the restaurant, but now I want to know everything."

Yikes.

He was right. I'd successfully veered us away from having this conversation at the restaurant. But there was no avoiding the subject now.

Here goes nothing.

Trying to sound light and breezy, like a carefree girl should, I said, "That's one tall order, Noel from Nevada. Where should I start?"

"How about telling me where you're from in Arizona?"

I saw no sense in lying since where I lived was so tiny and insignificant it hardly made a blip on the map.

Taking a breath, I exhaled slowly and replied, "I live in a tiny town called Two Palms."

"Huh." Noel appeared thoughtful. "I've never heard of it."

"I'm not surprised. Not many people have."

"What kind of work do you do there, Maisie? Do you have a job?"

I wasn't about to tell him I worked part-time at a local convenience store, as it would ruin the image I was carefully crafting.

So instead, I said, "I'm in school."

I had taken two classes at the local community college recently, so it wasn't a total lie. Truth was I wanted so badly to get a degree and escape my crappy little town.

It was going to take forever, though, at the rate I was going.

Noel looked at me, assessing. "You do look pretty young. What are you? Twenty-one, twenty-two?"

"I'm twenty-one," I confirmed. "Why? How old are you?"

"Twenty-five," he replied.

Mock scandalized, I covered my mouth.

"Are you telling me I'm out with an older man? Say it isn't so!"

Noel laughed. And then he asked, "What's your major at school?"

Ugh, we were back to that.

"Business," I said.

"Hmm," he murmured.

I really wanted to move away from the subject before he pried too deeply. So I said in a rush, "How did you get into hockey, Noel from Nevada? You must've been pretty good right from the start to end up playing professionally."

"I was okay, I guess," he oh-so-humbly replied. "I was recruited right out of juniors, so I guess I was okay."

Being recruited out of juniors meant nothing to me, so I moved onto the next subject.

"I don't have any siblings," I began, to get my response out of the way immediately. "Do you have any brothers or sisters, though?"

"I do." He smiled happily, so I assumed they got along well. "I have a twin sister."

I was taken aback, but in a good way. Twins were cool.

"Wow, that's awesome," I said. "What's her name?"

"Noelle."

I couldn't help but laugh. Her name sounded so much like his.

"Sorry," I said, stifling another giggle.

Noel shrugged. "Ah, it's all right. We get that a lot. What can I say? We were born in December, and our parents *really* love the holidays."

"They do?"

"Hell yeah they do. You should see how my folks do up our house every year, the one we grew up in back in Chicago. During the holidays, it's the talk of the neighborhood."

I thought about how my mom hadn't even bothered to put up a tree last year. And how we'd heated up burritos I brought home from the convenience store on Christmas day for our holiday dinner.

Noel, conversely, led the perfect life.

Not only was he a successful hockey player, but I could tell from the way he talked about his family that they meant a lot to him, especially his twin sister.

He'd probably run far, far away from me if he knew I had the kind of mom who dragged her daughter to a foreign country, only to abandon her there for a guy.

Taking a deep breath, I blinked back traitorous tears welling in my eyes.

Shit, not now!

Noel, nice guy that he so clearly was, noticed immediately.

"Hey, hey…" He got up and sat down on the end of my chair. "What's wrong? Did I say something to upset you?"

"No, no. I'm fine."

He took my hand. "Maisie, seriously, you're not fine. You're crying. So something's not right." He took a breath, and added, "You can talk to me if you want."

I wanted so badly to believe him.

I wanted to come clean.

But I couldn't.

Sniffling, I said, "Suffice it to say, my life growing up was much different than yours."

Noel seemed to realize I didn't want to say much more on the subject, and he didn't press for details.

He simply said, "I'm sorry, Maisie."

Despite his kindness, I felt embarrassed and vulnerable. This was not how the night was supposed to go. I was way off-track.

Scoffing, I bit out, "I'm a rotten date, aren't I?"

Noel moved his hand from mine, placing his warm palm tenderly to my cheek.

"No, you're not a rotten date," he said. "Not at all. I'm the one who upset you, so if anyone's ruining the night, it's me."

This guy.

"You're too sweet, Noel from Nevada."

He went on to say something more, but I was done talking. I had to do something, make some kind of a dramatic move, before I became too emotional and freaking blew my cover.

So I sat up, pressed my lips to his, and started kissing the crap out of Noel from Nevada.

10

NOT LIKE ANYONE ELSE

NOEL

Whoa, Maisie.

Before I knew what was happening, she leaned forward and started kissing me. And these were not tender pecks. As soon as our lips met, it became a desperate, hot, mind-blowing make-out session.

We were on the same chair, so I pulled her into my lap.

Maisie straddled me, her dress riding up.

Clearly, she was no longer upset.

This woman sure was keeping me on my toes.

I liked it, though.

And I was right there with her, my lips parting hers, our tongues touching.

Fuck.

She was honeysuckles, warmth, and the promise of wild sex.

I wanted more, so I stopped kissing her long enough to ask, "Should we go down to my room?"

She looked torn, but said, "Uh, okay."

I was about to pick her up and carry her inside, where I planned to have her in so many fucking ways. But I started having second thoughts.

I mean, I liked Maisie. And I didn't want her doing something she didn't really want to do.

So I gave her an out by softly saying, "We don't *have* to go inside. I'm pretty happy just kissing you right here."

She smiled at me sweetly. "I am too, actually."

I touched my lips to hers. "So we'll stay out here, maybe make out a little more?"

She smiled against my mouth. "Yes, Noel from Nevada, I think I'd like that."

"Good. Then it's decided."

I went back to kissing her, though much more softly, like I was cherishing her with my mouth, which I definitely was.

My dick wasn't too happy with the turn of events, and he took the time to remind me that Maisie had been the one to basically attack me.

She wants it bad, man, he taunted. *She's just playing coy. No one is around. Let's just fuck her right here in the chair.*

I knew better than to listen to that bastard. He pretty much had a one-track mind.

One of these days, though, I did want to hike up Maisie's hot little dress and bury myself in her sure-to-be sweet pussy.

But it wouldn't be tonight, as I wanted her to be 100% onboard.

We kissed a while longer, until we had to cool things down.

Otherwise, we *would* end up back in my room.

Settling back in the chair, I encircled Maisie in my arms.

She twisted around, peering up at me, her indigo eyes dark and sad.

"What's up?" I asked, brow rising.

"It's just…" She seemed to be fighting to find the right words. "You're a nice guy, Noel. Aren't you?"

I wasn't sure why that would be such a bad thing, but she didn't look particularly happy about it for some reason.

"I try to be," I replied. "Why? Would you rather I wasn't?"

She seemed to snap out of whatever sad funk she was in, and exclaimed, "Oh, no. I didn't mean it like that. Not at all. It's just that I haven't met many guys like you."

"Is that a good thing, or a bad thing?" I queried, just to double-check.

Laying her head down on my chest, she murmured, "It's definitely a good thing. Trust me on that one."

I kissed the top of her head, and started rubbing her back. "You're pretty nice yourself, Maisie from Arizona."

"Ha," she snorted. "I don't know about that."

"Well, you're certainly unique. Can we at least go with that?"

Tracing a little heart over my pec, she said, "Okay. But just like you asked me, is that a good or a bad thing?"

"It's good, Maisie. Unique is good. Very, very good."

It was too. Maisie was not only beautiful, she was quirky, spontaneous, and fun.

And she was a bit of a mystery.

One I couldn't wait to figure out.

A LETDOWN AND AN INVITATION

MAISIE

Despite my meltdown, I truly had enjoyed my date with Noel.

He'd really gone all out to show me a good time, and it had paid off. I'd had a super evening.

The kissing on the rooftop alone was *gah*.

Yeah, that was definitely the best, as Noel Sandlund was an extraordinary kisser.

When I went back to my room that night, all the emotion and sexual energy caught up to me. I was so freaking hot and bothered that I could barely stand it.

So, shedding my dress, I drew a hot bath. And then I proceeded to get off three times under the warm running water from the faucet.

Stockholm had surprisingly great water pressure.

Who knew?

I slept really well that night, no surprise there.

In the morning, however, I awoke with a start, remembering that what I was building with Noel wasn't real.

He was simply a means to an end.

Too bad my heart was protesting like crazy. I genuinely liked the guy. And a part of me, a big part, wished I could explore the possibilities. I mean, damn, Noel and I got along so beautifully. And we were extremely attracted to one another. I would have hopped into bed with him in a heartbeat last night, but since I was playing the long game, I knew it was prudent to take things slowly.

Still, it was all becoming too much. This wasn't me. I didn't cheat and lie to get what I wanted. Maybe my mother did, but I was different.

Suddenly, I was furious—at her, at me, at life.

"Fuck!" I ground out, hitting the pillow with my fist.

I hated that my mom had put me in this position. Speaking of Parent of the Year, I decided I should to try and get a hold of her. Maybe she'd spoken to Gary and had finally procured me that plane ticket home.

If that were the case, I could quit playing games with Noel. I could start to date him for real, no agendas.

But would he really want a girl like you?

Haven't we been over this?

I sighed, hating the voices of doubt that were chiming in my mind.

But they were right. Noel and I were from completely different worlds.

Like, I could never afford to stay in a hotel like this on my own.

But he could.

He clearly assumed I was from money.

A college student who had funds to travel internationally with her friend, and then when the said friend leaves, she stays on?

Those were definitely the actions of a carefree girl with cash to blow.

Ha, if only.

I'd told Noel I was "playing it by ear," further cultivating the fun girl image.

Yeah, right.

My life was not even close to fun and carefree. I was staying in Stockholm because I had no other choice.

Although I had to admit that I didn't hate it nearly as much, not since I'd met Noel.

If it weren't so sad, my situation would be funny.

My melancholy mood from last night returned with a vengeance, and worsened when I got ahold of my mom.

She told me right off it wasn't a good time, and that she'd just "talk to me later."

"Wait," I called out, praying she hadn't already disconnected. "I only wanted to ask if you've talked to the Juice King about getting me that plane ticket home."

Mom huffed.

Hey, at least she was still there.

"Maisie, I told you not to call him that. He prefers to be called Gary."

"Whatever," I snapped, not ever remembering her saying that. "Did you talk to him or not?"

"I will, Maisie. I told you I would."

I groaned.

That meant no, she had not talked to him.

I sighed. "When do you plan to bring it up?"

Sounding even more irritated with me, she said, "I don't know. But I'll call you when I do, okay? Speaking of which, it's probably better if you don't call me again. We've been very busy lately. And like I said before, I can't talk now. We're in Rome and about to go sightseeing. Gary just ran to the men's room for a sec, but he'll be back any minute."

"Rome?" I yelped. "Where are you staying? Do you have a hotel name or number? What if I need to reach you and your cell's not on?"

Too late, Mom was done giving out info.

Wearily, she said, "Goodbye, Maisie."

"Mom, no… Hold up a sec, please."

It was too late. She was gone.

I was still in the same position of having to rely on myself to get home.

That, unfortunately, meant I had no choice but to continue my farce with Noel.

"That man is going to hate me so much when this is all done," I lamented.

I was sure I'd hate myself even more. Hell, I was halfway there now.

Noel and I hadn't made any specific plans when we'd wrapped up last night, so I was surprised when my cell rang and I saw that it was him.

I thought maybe I'd scared him off with my emotional breakdown.

But no, there was his name on my screen.

Oh my God, my heart was fluttering.

"Hey," I answered, returning to my carefree façade. "Missing me already?"

Noel chuckled.

Oh, how I already loved his sexy laugh.

"Actually, I *was* missing you, Maisie from Arizona."

I also loved his candor.

"Hmm, I see your charm game is still going strong today, Noel from Nevada."

"It is. But is it working?"

Coyly, I replied, "I don't know. I'll tell you in a minute."

"How about you tell me later today instead?" Noel proposed. "Are you busy this afternoon?"

"I don't know," I hedged. "I'll have to check my planner. I may have a hot date with the hotel bartender."

"You better not," Noel growled.

Oooh, feisty Noel.

I liked this one too.

He was trying to give the impression he was kidding around, but there was a definite edge to his tone.

That was fine.

I liked that he cared.

And it thrilled me to think he was a little jealous, as well.

So I decided to push it a bit, see how much he really did care.

"No, for real, Noel," I stated very seriously. "The other night that flirty bartender asked me out. It was right before you came over. I'm sure that's why he was giving you dirty looks the rest of the evening."

"Maisie," Noel warned, "I really hope what you're telling me isn't true."

"If it were, would it bother you?"

Softly, he admitted, "I think you know that it would."

I couldn't torture the poor guy any longer, so I confessed.

"I'm just kidding around, okay? The bartender didn't really ask me out, and even if he had I probably would've said no. After last night, I definitely would have declined."

He blew out a clearly relieved breath.

"Thank God. You don't know how good that makes me feel."

My heart soared.

Noel definitely liked me.

And I liked him.

But wait, I shouldn't.

This wasn't real.

So why does it feel so real, Maisie?

Ugh!

Getting back on track, before another misplaced meltdown occurred, I asked, "So what's this afternoon?"

"Team USA is playing in a semifinal game. It's against Team Sweden. That means the arena will be rockin'. So would you want to go?"

Go watch Noel Sandlund play hockey?

Was he kidding?

I wasn't much of a fan of the sport before, but I sure was now.

"Hell, yeah!" I exclaimed. "I'd love to go."

"Excellent."

"Cool."

He sounded as excited as I when he said, "Okay. I have to ride over to the arena on a bus with the team, but I can leave you a ticket at the box office."

"Great, that works. I'll just take a cab or an Uber over to the arena, no problem."

"Would you want to meet up after the game? We could go out and grab a light bite to eat, or whatever."

He was so cute.

"Yes, a bite to eat sounds like fun."

"Then it's settled?"

"Yep, sounds good."

Noel told me where to meet him—in a lounge down near the locker rooms.

"I'll be sure to have a pass in with the ticket," he said. "That'll allow you access to the lounge and locker room area."

"Perfect." I nodded, even though he couldn't see me. "I can't wait."

"Me too, Maisie. I'm pumped to see you again."

"Aww…"

We wrapped up a minute later, and I lay there in bed, thinking.

I couldn't believe I was pumped for, of all things, a hockey game.

But it wasn't just any ole hockey game. It was a semifinal match between Team USA and Team Sweden.

And yes, I'd be rooting for my country's team.

But mostly, I'd be rooting for Noel.

12

YOU WIN SOME, YOU LOSE SOME

NOEL

It was the final ten minutes of play in the semifinal game, and Team USA was down by one goal.

Shit, we have to tie this thing up or we're fucking done.

It was true. Whoever won this game would advance to the finals. And the loser would go home.

I was thinking all this during a timeout that was due to a chewed-up section of ice. It was dangerous and needed to be repaired before play could resume.

While the ice crew worked on taking care of the issue, I skated along the boards to center ice, where Maisie was seated. I'd procured her an awesome spot up along the glass.

It'd been great for me too, having given me multiple opportunities during the game to check her out.

Man, did she ever look gorgeous tonight. Tight jeans, a snug black sweater, and a big colorful scarf she'd tied up in some fancy twist, my girl was stunning.

We hadn't had a chance to interact, but since this was a longer than usual break, I stopped in front of where she was.

Too bad there was still only enough time for her to wave and smile at me.

I tapped the glass with my stick in response, and then it was time for the game to resume.

Maisie gave me a thumbs-up as I skated away backward. When the game started back up, I was more pumped than ever to show off my skill.

Right away, there was a chance.

With a lot of back-and-forth action up and down the ice, it felt like we were on the verge of scoring. But then a bunch of stupid shit happened.

First, Blake missed a perfect pass from me.

That didn't occur often.

We were just off.

Seconds later, I had a good scoring chance, but my shot hit the post.

Fuck.

A player on our team then got burned for misreading a play, allowing Team Sweden to score.

Double fuck.

They were now up by two.

We sure had our work cut out for us.

We had another chance to score when an opposing forward blatantly hooked Blake. The offending player got called for the infraction, and our team went on a power play.

Yes!

Er, maybe not.

As soon as our one-man advantage began, Team Sweden's defense boxed us out. We started losing battles all over the place.

"Come on, damn it!" I yelled at my own guys when the other team obtained possession for the third time in less than forty seconds. "We're the ones on the power play, remember?"

It was true. We were supposed to be the team in control. We had the extra man advantage, right?

Oh, but it got worse from there.

Even though we soon had a two-man advantage, once our goaltender was pulled, we fell apart.

It all started when I skated down the ice to retrieve a loose puck, clearly icing by the other team.

When I touched the puck, though, the ref waved the icing call off.

What?

I yelled at him, "Are you fucking kidding me? We're on the power play, bud. And that was clearly icing by the other team."

While I was jawing at the official, one of Team Sweden's goons came up from behind me and boarded my ass.

"Oof." I went down.

The ref let that go too, probably because of my yapping.

Great.

While I was down on the ice, the fucking goon took the opportunity to flick the puck into our empty net.

Nooooo!

Team Sweden had just scored another goal.

Time ran out seconds later, and the horn sounded.

The game was over.

We had lost.

The spectators, of course, went crazy. We were in Sweden and their country's team had just won an important game.

I was so pissed that I slammed my stick on the ice, breaking it in two.

Blake skated over.

"Come on, Sandlund," he said. "Don't let your frustration show. Don't give the crowd that kind of satisfaction."

I blew out a breath. "I know. You're right. It's just that this is complete bullshit."

I was so mad.

"Eh." Blake shrugged. "What can you do? You win some, you lose some."

We started skating over to the runway to head down to the locker room, and I sighed. "Yeah, I guess. It just sucks that the Wolves were knocked out of the playoffs early, and now Team USA is done too."

"I hear ya, man. It's back to New York for me. And who knows how long I'll even be there."

He was right. The Rangers had a ton of big contracts coming up, and one of those was Blake's. It was highly likely he'd be traded over the summer. I was kind of hoping the Wolves would pick him up.

But we'd have to see.

Before I left the ice, I looked around for Maisie. She was gone, probably on her way down to the lounge area to wait for me.

That was the only good thing about my so-far crappy day. I was excited to spend time with her. I knew she could help me forget about the shitty game.

The thought of Maisie made me consider what my next step would be now that Team USA was done.

Would I fly home to Las Vegas?

Hmm, I wasn't so sure.

Maisie was here, and probably would be for a while, seeing as she was "playing it by ear."

Maybe I'd just do the same.

Down in the locker room, after discarding my equipment and taking a quick shower, I threw on some boxer briefs, dark-wash jeans, and a long-sleeved olive-green pullover.

And then I went out to look for the woman who was about to become my reason for staying in Sweden for the rest of the summer.

Or for however long it took to get her to fall for me.

It seemed fair, seeing as I was falling for her.

13

HE'S STAYING, SO WHY WOULD I GO?

MAISIE

For someone whose team had just been beaten, Noel was in a surprisingly upbeat mood.

When I asked him what was up with that, he told me his positive attitude had something to do with me.

"*Now* you have to tell me what's going on," I declared.

As our ride pulled up, he said, "Okay, but first let's get in the car."

It wasn't really a "car." Noel had once again rented a limo for us to tool around in for the night.

"Is this your usual go-to transportation?" I asked with a laugh when the limo driver jumped out and opened the door for me.

As I slid in and across the soft leather seat, making room for Noel, he replied, "Yes, this actually is my go-to transportation for when I'm taking you out here in Sweden."

I murmured a soft but heartfelt, "You're sweet, Noel from Nevada."

"Well, Maisie from Arizona," he murmured back, "that's nice of you to say. For the record, though, if we were back in the States, *I'd* be doing the driving."

"Oh, is that so?" I laughed. "Aren't you Mr. Chivalrous?"

Chuckling, he replied, "I'm trying to be."

I raised a curious brow. "What do you drive, anyway?"

He replied, "A Porsche Panamera."

"Wow, nice."

It was nice, as in *it must be nice.* I had nothing.

We started on our way to dinner, and Noel, of course, asked, "What do you drive?"

Uh-oh.

"Um, I…"

I couldn't tell him I had no car, as it'd ruin my carefully crafted illusion.

So I hastily blurted out, "I'm kind of in between vehicles right now."

Accepting that, he said, "Exploring your options, huh?"

Ha!

"Something like that."

Hell, I had no options. It was pretty simple, really—no money equaled no car.

Needing to change the subject before the truth slipped out, I said, "So you still haven't told me why you're so upbeat when your team just lost a big game. You said it had something to do with me?"

He nodded. "It sure does."

"How so?"

Noel reached over and took my hand. I let him because I liked how warm and strong he always felt.

I could get used to this.

Looking into my eyes, his blues sparkling, he said, "I'm happy because you inspired me."

I couldn't help but laugh.

"*I* inspired *you*? Do tell, in what way?"

This I had to hear. It was probably a joke.

But Noel wasn't laughing when he said, "I've decided to stay on in Sweden. And it's because of you. I like your philosophy, Maisie from Arizona. I like your playing-it-by-ear attitude. Truth is, I need to learn to do a little more of that myself."

God, if he only knew the truth.

But I couldn't exactly come clean.

So I nodded dumbly and said, "Wow, that's great."

It was great in some ways. Like it gave me more time to work on Noel. I still needed to get him to like me enough to buy me a ticket home.

But then again, I wasn't so sure I even wanted a ticket home, at least not any time soon. If Noel was staying in Sweden, I wanted to stick around too.

Yes, I wanted to spend as much time as possible with Noel Sandlund. This wasn't really a means to an end, not anymore.

I really liked him.

Heaven help me.

14

TAKING IT DAY BY DAY

NOEL

Once I had decided to stay in Stockholm, it felt like the best decision I'd made in a long time.

Fuck, it was amazing to take life just day-by-day.

I didn't care anymore about Team USA having lost in the world championships. To me it just meant I had more time to spend with Maisie.

And that's what we did.

Over the next couple of weeks, she and I hung out *a lot*.

We went to dinner, had drinks at the bar, and walked around Stockholm almost every evening. We also took in a few movies that were playing in English.

I even took her ice skating once.

Trust me, once was enough, as it turned out to be quite the adventure.

Maisie had never skated prior to that day, and she spent most of her time falling down on the ice.

That was okay.

She didn't get hurt, and afterward I got to warm her up, which involved lots of kissing.

Damn, our make-out sessions were the best.

But it was becoming clearer and clearer that both of us wanted—and needed—more.

Since the night up on the hotel rooftop, when Maisie was so torn about going back to my room, I'd made the decision to back way the fuck off.

I wanted to be careful with her heart, because I really liked her.

But now it was time to move things to the next level.

Still, I wanted our first time to be something really special.

That's what inspired me to plan an overnight trip for us to Oslo, Norway.

I knew it would be the perfect place to consummate our relationship. Maisie and I were spending so much time in Stockholm that it was becoming way too familiar to us.

Our first time happening there wouldn't feel special enough.

So Oslo it was.

Maisie was into it as soon as I brought the idea up to her. Though I didn't tell her I was planning on devouring her there. I'd play that by ear, making sure the time really was right.

She deserved perfection.

"Let's rent a car and drive across Sweden," I said. "We can cross the border into Norway and stay in Oslo. What do you think?"

"I love that idea!" Maisie exclaimed. "A road trip sounds great. I want to see Norway. One thing, though."

"Anything, babe," I replied.

"As soon as we get to Oslo, we have to go to Frogner Park. I've seen so many pictures, and it looks *so* cool."

"Wait." I chuckled. "I've seen a few pictures too. Isn't that the park with all the nude sculptures?"

Maisie chastised, "Noel."

I laughed. "It is, isn't it?"

"Yes," Maisie confirmed, with a roll of her eyes.

"Well, anything naked and I'm in." I waggled my brows suggestively, though it was all in fun.

Still, Maisie whacked my arm. "Be serious, Noel. It's not some perv attraction. It's art depicting life."

"Oh, is that so?"

"Yes. I read in a magazine article a while back that the statues were sculpted nude so as not to lock them into any one time period. They're ageless that way, and have more impact when you see them."

The park actually did sound really interesting. And her explanation made sense.

I was just kidding around, anyway.

I told her as much and promised we'd definitely go to the park.

One thing I kept to myself was that Maisie may have been excited to see nude statues, but I was far more pumped at the thought of finally seeing *her* without clothes.

15

OSLO

MAISIE

Oslo was super cool. It was a cosmopolitan city, ultra-sleek and more modern than I expected.

"I like it here," I declared to Noel as we drove into the city.

"Already," he laughed. "We've only been here for five minutes, Mais."

"It doesn't matter." I shrugged. "I know what I feel. And Oslo feels like my kind of town."

"Well, then it's settled." He smiled over at me. "I like it too. So tell me more about it."

I had a guide book on my lap that we'd picked up at a rest stop while still in Sweden. I'd been reading Noel random Oslo facts and tidbits for the past hour. And I was more than ready to regale him with more.

As we traveled through the downtown to our hotel, I looked around, noting we were perfectly angled that to our left was what the guide book touted as "an interesting part of the Oslo skyline."

Pointing that way, I said to Noel, "Look over there. Check out those buildings. See how they're built in a straight line, but stand at all varying heights?"

Scrunching down and peering over, he said, "Yeah, that's cool. I see what you mean."

"It says here," I went on, "those are known as the 'barcode' buildings."

"Huh." He took another quick look. "Wow, you're right. Lined up like that, they really do look like a giant barcode on the skyline."

"It's pretty cool, right?"

"Very cool, Maisie, very cool. And for the record, I like learning these little facts with you."

He smiled over at me, and I grinned back.

Noel was obviously enjoying our excursion as much as I was. That made me so freaking happy.

He looked amazing today too, like always. His blond hair was slicked back, making his face more chiseled than ever.

He had such an amazing face; I never tired of looking at it.

It was also neat that we'd unintentionally dressed alike. Both of us had on faded distressed jeans and black long-sleeved tees.

Feeling close to Noel, I reached over and placed my hand on his thigh.

"I'm having such a good time already," I said softly. "I'm glad we're doing this."

"I am too, Maisie. It feels great to get away with you."

"It does," I agreed. "This really feels special."

"It does."

Noel peered over at me pointedly, and I knew then that he meant more than just us enjoying Oslo. It'd been left unsaid, but both of us were ready for more physically.

We'd progressed slowly to this point, mainly due to me, but it was finally time to take things to the next level.

I wanted more too. I just wanted the timing to be right. I had a feeling, though, that it would be soon.

Oslo just felt right.

After checking into the hotel, Noel kept good on his promise and drove us straight over to Frogner Park.

On first glance, many of the Vigeland sculptures did indeed appear strange.

Like, there was a giant man statue juggling babies, and one of a toddler throwing a temper tantrum. That one prompted Noel to make several funny comments.

Leaning in, he murmured, "That kid looks like some of my teammates when they miss a shot."

I burst out laughing. "Do they really get *that* mad? 'Cause that baby looks pissed as hell."

He assured me, "Some of the players really do get pissed like that. I kid you not. Of course, *I* would never behave that way."

Chuckling, and thinking about the semi-final game where Noel broke his stick in two, I said, "Oh, no, of course *you* would never be like that."

I had appreciated his passion that day, though. I couldn't wait to see it expressed in *other* ways.

As we strolled through the park, I surmised the sculptures really were quite genius. Ones that at first appeared strange were anything but when put into context.

As I'd read in that magazine article, many of the themes dealt with the circle of life, including love and relationships. Those were the ones that made me think about my relationship with Noel. As I had realized a few days prior, it was no longer about procuring a plane ticket home.

It hadn't been for a while.

I truly cared for the guy.

And I knew he felt the same way about me.

That's when it hit me—I *had* to come clean.

There was no choice anymore.

So I made a decision then and there I would tell Noel the truth, the whole truth. I'd share the story of how I'd come to be deserted in Stockholm thanks to my mother, and how I wasn't really a carefree tourist. I'd tell him I wasn't much of a college student, either. That I'd only ever taken two classes.

I'd also come clean about how I lived in a trailer, and that I couldn't afford a car.

Hard as it would be, I'd admit I only took an interest in him originally to scam a plane ticket back home.

But I'd make sure he knew that I no longer felt that way.

I cared for him deeply.

In fact, I was falling for Noel Sandlund.

Or had I already fallen?

Shit, did I love him?

As I stood there, staring blankly at one of the park's showpieces, a giant obelisk of people reaching and clambering toward something bigger than themselves—*how fitting*—Noel touched my arm.

"Maisie, are you all right? You look like you're really feeling bothered by something."

I shook my head.

It wasn't the right time to get into any of this.

I said, "No, I'm fine," then took a breath.

"You sure?"

"Yeah, but is it okay if we head back to the hotel now? There's something I need to talk to you about."

"Sure, that's fine." He glanced at his watch. "We should head back over there, anyway."

"Why's that?" I asked, curious as to what was up.

Smiling at me slyly, Noel said, "There's something I want you to see back in our room."

I had no idea what he was up to, but I was curious to find out.

Maybe I was just using that curiosity to delay the inevitable talk we needed to have.

Whatever the case, I decided that for now I'd hold off on my big confession.

16

MAKING HER MINE

NOEL

was anxious to find out what Maisie wanted to talk about. She
sounded so serious. But I hoped it could wait a little while.

I had a really romantic evening planned back at our hotel. At
least, I hoped it would turn out that way. I'd certainly taken the steps
to make it so.

While we were at the park, checking out the naked statues, the
housekeeping staff, on my direction, was decking out the hotel room
with fragrant fresh flowers and dozens of candles. I'd also requested
they leave bubble bath and big fuzzy robes in the bathroom for us.

We had a huge tub that fit two, so why not take advantage of it?

If all went as planned, I'd finally take Maisie to bed tonight.

But now I wasn't so sure.

On our way back to the hotel, things weren't looking too promising.

Maisie was being unusually quiet. I assumed it had something to do with whatever it was she wanted to talk about.

"Ah, hell…" Instead of tabling any discussion for later, I just flat-out asked, "What did you want to talk to me about, Maisie? Maybe we should just address it now."

"Oh?"

She sounded surprised I'd brought it up. I guess that was why she suddenly backpedaled.

"It was nothing really," she said in a rush. "It can definitely wait."

I paused for a second, and then said, "Are you sure? You're being really quiet over there, kind of like there might be something heavy weighing on your mind."

Maisie waved me off, looking nervous as she did.

"No, no. I'm just thinking. That's all."

I felt compelled to press, asking, "About what?"

She seemed to scramble for an answer, eventually saying, "Um, I was just wondering what you have up your sleeve for when we get back to the hotel."

Hmm, I doubted that was it. But I sensed it'd be wise to let a potentially serious discussion drop for the time being.

So, winking over at her, I said, "Ah, you'll find out soon enough."

"I can't wait."

The mood lightened then, and we talked and laughed about the fun we'd had at the park. I was just happy Maisie was back to her usual self. I was also pumped she was clearly feeling rather frisky. She was leaning over and kissing my cheek, my neck, and other parts.

By the time we were back at the hotel, Maisie was all over me.

"Wow." I chuckled as we made our way through the hotel lobby to the elevators, amid a few curious stares. "Those statues really worked you up, huh?"

She stopped groping me, removing her hand from my ass long enough to snort, "Hmpff. Would you prefer I stopped touching you?"

"No, no, not at all." I whisked her into the elevator, encircling her in my arms. "You just keep on doing what you're doing, babe."

"Mmm, I think I will."

Once the elevator doors closed and we were ascending to our floor, we kissed and groped with abandon. We were both heated to the boiling point by the time we reached our room.

I couldn't wait to get Maisie undressed and under me. I was in such a fog of lust that I actually almost forgot about the arrangements I'd made.

But I remembered the second we stepped into the room.

How could I not?

The aroma of flowers punctuated the air, and the whole room was aglow with the light of dozens of candles.

"Wow, Noel…" Maisie pulled away from me and spun around in a little circle. "I love this. Did you have the hotel staff do this while we were out?"

"I did," I replied sheepishly.

She turned to me, brow arched. "No wonder you were up for going to the park right away."

I laughed, walking over to her. "That wasn't my sole reason for going to the park. You made me interested when you said there'd be nude statues, remember?"

"Ha, ha." She swatted my arm. "Stop kidding around."

I couldn't help but smile. "Okay. But I am glad you like all of this."

I followed her eyes as she took another sweeping perusal of the romantic room.

"I just can't believe you set it all up for me," she murmured.

"I did, Mais. I did."

"Oh, Noel…" Rising to her tiptoes, she wrapped her arms around me. "You are far too good to me."

I lowered my lips to hers, and murmured, "Only because you deserve the best, babe."

"You say that a lot," she sighed.

"Only because it's true."

I kissed her again, this time while backing her toward the bed.

Once we reached the mattress's edge, we toppled onto the downy soft comforter.

A few seconds were spent scooting up to the pillows, but then we got back down to the business of making out.

Kissing, kissing, and not coming up for air.

Who needed air when you were subsisting on love?

The significance of that passing thought was lost on me in the heat of the moment. Even though we made out all the time, this was… different. We both knew there'd be no more holding back.

Lifting my body from Maisie, I popped open the button on her jeans and lowered the zipper.

Looking down at her, I raised a brow. "Should I keep going?"

She nodded, so I lifted her top to just above her sexy black bra. The lacy edge of the silky cups called to me to just tear the damn thing off. But I held back. If it had been any other woman, I wouldn't have.

But this was Maisie, and I wanted to take my time with her.

Not to mention, I kind of liked the way her rolled-up top was squeezing her breasts together. It looked super sexy.

Taking her in, I breathed out a raspy, "You are so fucking hot, Maisie from Arizona."

Reaching up, she caressed my stubbled cheek. "You're pretty hot yourself, Noel from Nevada."

I cupped her breast, murmuring, "The things I want to do to you…"

"So do them," she urged.

Yeah, do them, my cock concurred.

I slid my hand down to her flat stomach, splaying my fingers wide as I marveled, "You are so damn soft."

Everything about this woman called to me as a male.

And she knew it.

Smiling wickedly, she slid her hand down my abs to my groin.

Cupping my erection through my jeans, Maisie groaned, "Hmm, I may be soft, but you're hard as fuck, Noel."

"It's because of you. I'm hard for you."

I wanted her hand on me bare, not through the fucking jeans. And I got my wish when Maisie yanked down the zipper and slid her hand under my boxer briefs.

"Fuck, yeah," I groaned.

Toying with the head of my cock, she circled and teased. And I grew longer and harder.

When she full-on grasped me, I ground out a ragged, "Don't stop."

But Maisie did stop, only so she could say, "I want to do something for you, Noel. Before anything else happens."

Confused, I muttered, "Huh, what?"

I was clearly gone, my head mush. Good thing Maisie had control of the situation.

Shimmying down the bed and angling her head to where I lifted, she rasped, "I've wanted to do this for so long."

Shit.

It wasn't like I was going to fight "this."

My jeans were already halfway down my ass, so Maisie had only to let go of me long enough to yank the denim down the rest of the way, along with my boxer briefs.

My cock sprang free, and her hot mouth was on me instantly.

"Jesus, Maisie. Damn."

The things she did with her tongue, the way her full lips wrapped around me, I was in heaven.

But the one thing I didn't want was for this to end too soon.

And it would if I let her continue.

With great reluctance, urging her head back, I murmured, "Hold up a sec."

Flopping onto my back, I tugged her up on to me.

"Why'd you stop me?" she asked.

Caressing her raven hair away from her face, I touched my fingers to her swollen lips.

"I loved everything you were doing, trust me, babe. But now it's my turn."

17

TOTAL BLISS

MAISIE

Noel said it was his turn, so who was I to deny him?

I wasn't sure how he'd done it—the man was freaking skilled—but in no time my jeans, my panties, my bra, and my long-sleeved tee were all off and on the floor.

I was on my back, knees spread wide, with Noel's head between my legs.

"Holy crap, you don't mess around," I gasped.

He laughed, his warm breaths teasing at my folds. "You ain't seen nothin' yet, babe."

He wasn't kidding.

He sucked my clit into his warm mouth, his tongue doing amazing things, making me cry out, "Yes!"

For as skilled as Noel was in taking off my clothes, he was a master at pleasing me with his mouth.

He took his time, licking me languorously, parting me, and straight-up fucking me with his tongue.

I came not once, but twice.

No, wait, make that three times.

I was at Noel's mercy, putty in his hands, by the time he kissed his way up my body to my lips.

"Kiss me, Maisie," he demanded. "I'm not done with you yet."

I liked this totally in-control Noel.

He lowered his body down to mine, our lips entangled as his hard cock pushed into my hip. I groaned and he readjusted, till he was right the fuck *there*.

I wanted more, and fast, so I shifted until the crown of his dick was pressed almost into me.

Noel pulled back slightly, and chuckled.

"Maisie, is there something you want?"

"Don't be a tease." I circled my hips, his length rubbing against my clit and over my entrance again and again.

"Look who's talking," he said.

I picked up the pace, breathing out, "I want you so much. I'm not teasing. Can't you tell?"

"I can," he purred.

"So take me. Slide your cock into me and fuck me hard."

"Jesus." He pressed his forehead to mine. "I should go get a condom first, though, yes?"

"You don't have to," I breathed out, my hips circling faster and faster. "I'm on birth control to keep my cycles regular. And I'm clean."

"So am I," he shared.

"Then take me, Noel. Fuck m—"

He slammed up into me, hard.

"Unh…"

I welcomed the intrusion as Noel pounded into me, meeting him with every forceful thrust.

It was better than I'd expected.

And my expectations had been high.

This, though, this was on a whole new level.

Being with Noel was nothing short of bliss, and I wanted it to never end.

Because of that, I decided to scrap my plan for coming clean.

Sure, I'd tell him the whole truth eventually, just…later.

18

BEYOND ALL EXPECTATIONS

NOEL

I wanted to stay in Oslo forever.

No, I wanted to remain in the hotel room there forever—with Maisie, just loving her.

But we didn't have forever.

Not even close.

We had only that one night.

But since neither of us could bear leaving early in the morning, I called down to the front desk and arranged for an extremely late checkout.

"As late as you can make it," I told the employee.

Maisie and I were still in bed, having left only for bathroom breaks.

When I hung up, her head resting on my smooth chest, Maisie asked, "How long do we have?"

"Until five o'clock. But I told them if we run over to just charge an extra day."

"Mmm, perfect."

I thought then about Maisie's desire to have a discussion, prompting me to ask, "Hey, what did you want to talk to me about yesterday?"

She looked confused at first, lifting her head and peering up at me with those deep indigo-blue eyes.

"What are you talking about?" she asked.

"Before we left the park, remember? You said you wanted to talk to me about something once we were back at the hotel."

"Oh, that…"

Oddly, I felt her tense up.

"Yes, that," I said.

"Ahh, it was nothing. I told you just to forget about it in the car, remember?"

"I remember. But are you sure?"

Maisie, nodding profusely, said, "Yes, uh-huh, I'm sure. I actually resolved it on my own, anyway. At least, I did for now."

"That sure was cryptic," I murmured.

Maisie did not reply.

Hmm, something was off. But I had no idea what it could be.

I would've pressed, but Maisie's stomach growled, reminding me that neither of us had eaten anything—besides each other, *hee hee*—since yesterday afternoon.

"Are you hungry, babe?" I asked.

She teased, "Hungry for you? Always, yes."

Her hand trailed down my abs, but before she could reach my cock, where we'd both lose control, I said, "Uh, I meant for real food."

I was up, in more ways than one, for continuing what she was starting. But I knew she needed sustenance other than me.

I was kind of due for some food too. I didn't want either of us passing out during one of our marathon sexual encounters.

Biting her lip contemplatively, Maisie replied, "Now that you mention it, I think I am a little hungry."

"Say no more." I reached over and grabbed the hotel phone with my free hand. "Let's order room service."

I proceeded to place an order for a breakfast of eggs, fruit, and an assortment of cheeses and croissants, big enough that we could share.

"How long did they say it'll take for the food to get up here?" Maisie asked after I hung up the phone.

"About twenty minutes," I told her.

"Then let me go, Noel." She wiggled her still-trapped hand from mine. "There's plenty of time for a little fun."

I wasn't about to argue with her on that one.

We somehow made it out of the room by five, but it was no easy task. After we had eaten, we were so refreshed we went for yet another round of sexing.

Shit, I wanted Maisie all the fucking time now. I'd created a monster—me.

But she was just as bad.

"Did you ever expect it to be so good with us?" Maisie asked on our drive back to Stockholm.

"Well..." I glanced over at her, smirking. "I had a feeling it'd be pretty damn fantastic. But you're right, it was better than I expected. Being with you is fucking amazing."

"I feel the same way, Noel. In fact"—she reached over—"I can't stop freaking touching you."

"Hey, I'm not complaining."

Her hand trailed up my leg, and since I was wearing cargo shorts, my dick responded immediately.

"If you keep that up," I warned, "I'm going to take the next exit and find some lonely road out in the forest where I can fuck your brains out."

Laughing, she covered my cock with her hand and squeezed lightly.

"Is that a promise, Noel?"

"You bet your ass it is."

"In that case..." Maisie undid the button on my shorts, tugged down the zipper, and raised her brow in invitation. "Do it," she said.

When she licked her lips, I was done for.

We had just entered a heavily forested area, so there was no reason not to follow through.

I took the next exit.

And less than ten minutes later, Maisie and I were getting down and busy in the Swedish forest.

19

FLU BUG BLUES

MAISIE

When we returned to Stockholm, our sexy times continued. It seemed Noel and I just couldn't get enough of each other.

But everything ground to a screeching halt when I came down with a damn flu bug.

"Who gets sick in the middle of summer?" I lamented as I pressed my head back against a pile of pillows on Noel's bed.

Noel had insisted I stay in his room for as long as I felt unwell. That way, he said, he could take good care of me.

He was doing a fine job of it too.

Not only did I have extra pillows, but he'd managed to bribe the softest down comforter from housekeeping.

Noel was also good at keeping on top of ordering copious amounts of chicken broth for me from room service.

That was fine since I had no appetite for any kind of solid food.

Noel was attentive in other ways too. He had sponged me off the night before, and then helped me into my pajamas when I felt too sick to move.

He's such a sweetheart.

"Eh, it happens," he said. "Getting sick in the summer, that is."

He leaned forward and placed the back of his hand against my forehead.

"Yeah, I guess," I replied glumly.

Suddenly, Noel exclaimed, "Damn it, Maisie, I think your fever's up."

"Is it?" I asked.

"Yes. And I don't like that one bit. We better make sure it hasn't gone up *too* far."

Jumping up from the edge of the bed, Noel rushed over to the dresser to retrieve the overworked thermometer.

I was surprised it hadn't conked out on us yet.

"Taking my temperature *again*?" I sighed. "I doubt it's changed that much from the last time you took it. Seeing as that was, like, five minutes ago."

If it hadn't hurt so much, I would have rolled my eyes. But they were throbbing like crazy, along with pretty much the rest of me.

My exasperation was real, however. Noel had been checking to see if my fever had worsened almost continuously.

"We have to stay on top of this," he stated somberly as he stuck the thermometer in my mouth, effectively shutting me up. "If your temperature goes one iota over 101, I'm taking you to the hospital."

Yikes.

I absolutely did not want to go there. Noel would find out I had no insurance. Not to mention, I had no money to pay any medical bills.

So yeah, a hospital was a definite no-go.

I breathed a huge sigh of relief when it turned out my temperature was actually slightly *below* one hundred.

Phew!

"See." I tried to muster some enthusiasm. "I told you I was getting better. That's lower than the last reading."

Noel was not impressed.

"Hmm, we'll see about that. You're not out of the woods yet. Even 99 is still too high for my liking."

"Maybe you're right," I concurred, sinking back down into the pillows.

Despite trying to stay upbeat, I really did feel crappy.

"Do you want me to lie down next to you?" Noel asked when he saw how sad and pathetic I looked.

I absolutely did want him next to me, as it was comforting to have him close. But I had to decline for his sake.

"No, I don't want you to get sick too."

He laughed, and God, the little crinkles around his eyes that he got were so freaking cute.

Noel had on the same faded jeans he'd worn the day before, when I first fell ill and he started taking care of me. He'd changed his shirt, though, to a dark brown knit pullover. The material clung to his muscles, and the color contrasted nicely with his slicked-back blond hair.

"Maisie," he said, shaking his head amusedly. "I've been taking care of you for the past twenty-four hours straight. I think the I-don't-want-you-to-get-sick ship has sailed. I've been fully exposed to your germs."

He was probably right, so I said, "I kind of would like you to lie here next to me."

I patted the spot to my right.

Noel had slept on the sofa on the other side of the room the night before, but we were clearly both to the point of *fuck it.*

Noel lay down next to me, but he stayed on top of the covers. That was fine with me. I just wanted him near.

And I wanted to hear his voice.

So, curling up to him, I asked, "Can you tell me a story?"

THE STORY OF ME

NOEL

Maisie wanted a story?

Well, I could definitely give her one.

Kissing the top of her head, I said, "Okay, sweetheart. I'm not much of a storyteller, but I'll give it a try."

Letting out a contented hum, she murmured, "Mmm, any story will do."

"Okay, so here goes nothing… Once upon a time there was this little boy who had a twin. The little boy's name was Noel, and his sister was called Noelle. Their names were so similar because their crazy parents happened to be more into Christmas than most of the world."

Maisie surmised, "Aw, this is story about you, isn't it?"

"Yes, it is," I confirmed.

"I like it already, then."

"Cool. In that case, let's continue."

"I can't wait, Noel."

She was so amped it made me feel more into it.

"So," I went on, clearing my throat, "little Noel's parents liked to take him and his sister to the skating rink, one that was located in a park in Chicago, not far from their home. His sister liked the ice fine enough and she thought skating was fun, but little Noel freaking loved it. There was something about the feel of the ice beneath his skates, even the smell of the rink appealed to him. Maybe because, for the first time in his short life, he felt like he belonged somewhere."

"You belonged on the ice even back then," Maisie said.

Nodding thoughtfully, I agreed, "Yeah, I guess I did."

She peered up at me, looking very sleepy.

Good, the story was working.

I urged her head back down to my chest. "Rest, sweetheart. Let me get back to my tale."

"Okay."

"Little Noel liked the ice so much also because he wasn't that great at other things, like school. His sister had always been a natural in the classroom, excelling in pretty much every subject. Noelle was just so damn smart that it sometimes made Noel feel kind of lost."

"Aw, Noel—"

"No, it's okay." I smoothed back her raven hair. "This is where the story gets really good."

"Oh, go on." Maisie smiled against my chest.

"So this little boy's parents realized just how much their son liked ice skating. And that he was pretty good at it. They were supportive and let him go to the rink at every possible opportunity. They also enrolled him in peewee hockey. And the rest, as they say, is history."

"Tell me more," Maisie said.

"Okay. Well young Noel continued on to youth hockey. And that's when his life really changed. He discovered he was better than just good. He was fucking great. And people began to notice."

"Mmm," Maisie hummed.

I continued stroking her hair as I spoke in a calm voice. "Young Noel continued to play hockey, and as he did his confidence grew and grew. His parents were approached by scouts who felt their now-teenage son should go to a special boarding school where he could fully focus on hockey. Can you believe it? I was that damn good."

"I believe it, Noel."

Aw, my girl was the best.

"Anyway, his parents wanted their son to live out his dream, so they mortgaged their home. All so he could go to the best hockey school in the country."

Maisie asked, "So what happened next?"

"I went to that school."

"Yeah, school…" Maisie was conking out, which was good, as she needed the rest.

I felt rather tired myself, so I shortened the story to its conclusion.

"The boy worked as hard as he could. He wanted to be the best defenseman he could be. And he succeeded. He was drafted in the first round that year. The first big paycheck teenage-Noel received, he started paying his parents back. It was the least he could do for all they had done for him. And as time wore on, he ended up paying off their mortgage entirely. He also started giving money to his sister so she could follow *her* dream, which was to go to college."

Maisie had drifted off, so I lay there quietly.

But just as my eyes were closing, she suddenly asked, "Didn't you mention once that your sister goes to school in Las Vegas?"

I rubbed my eyes. "Yes. She lives there too. That's where she chose to go to college. She's in graduate school now, working on her MBA."

"Ah, got it."

Maisie yawned, making me yawn, and then she asked, "Is there more to your story, Noel? Like, what's the next chapter for you?"

Hmm, a really excellent question.

I'd devoted so much of my life to hockey, but things were different now. My story had taken a turn—a really good turn.

Something besides hockey was important to me, and that was Maisie.

When she asked again what my next chapter would be, I told her the truth. "I'm kind of working on that one right now. But I have to say it's looking pretty promising, like the next one might be the best chapter yet."

CONFESSION, TAKE ONE

MAISIE

Well, that woke me up.

I peered up at Noel, and he smiled down at me.

Did he just say what I think he said?

Yes, stupid, his next chapter is about you.

Crap, I needed to get this right.

Sighing, I said, "You deserve a happy-ever-after, Noel."

"As do you, sweetheart, as do you."

Ah, if only that were true.

I lowered my head back down to his chest, and he wrapped his arms around me. We were quiet then, as both of us had a lot to think about.

I knew I sure did.

I'd become a part of Noel's story, that much was clear. He said he was working on the next chapter, *his* next chapter.

But he'd become a part of my story too.

And that's when I realized that, along the way, I had freaking fallen head-over-heels in love with Noel from Nevada. No more maybes, this was it.

Problem was, I wasn't the Maisie from Arizona he thought me to be.

I was so much…less.

I knew then that I *had* to come clean. No more waiting or putting the "talk" on hold. If Noel cared for me in the same way I cared for him, then maybe, just *maybe*, he'd understand.

With my cheek pressed to his chest, I toyed with a loose thread on his pullover.

"Noel," I whispered. "I do have something I need to talk to you about. It's the same something I mentioned in Oslo."

I blew out a breath. This was going to be hard.

"Anyway, if you hate me forever once I say what I have to say, even if you kick me out of your room, I'll totally understand."

It was weird he wasn't saying anything. Maybe he was already mad just hearing that much.

Yikes.

Tentatively, my heart beating like a bird loose in my chest, I tilted my head back and ventured a peek up at him.

And that's when I had to laugh.

It was either that or cry.

Despite the fact Noel was sitting up and leaned back against the pillows, he was out like a light.

I wrapped my arms around this most amazing man. And since I knew he was asleep, it was safe to say out loud what was bursting in my heart.

"I love you so damn much, Noel from Nevada."

22

JUST DO IT, MAN

NOEL

had this really wild dream. In it, Maisie told me she loved me. And it made me so damn happy that I woke up.

Why did hearing that she loved me please me so much, though?

Did I love her back?

Maisie had become important to me, yes, but was that because I loved her?

Shit, I think so.

I looked down at her.

No, wait, I know I do.

I'd known it for a while now too. I just hadn't been ready to face it. But I was now.

I chuckled with a sense of happy relief. I did so lightly, though, since Maisie was sprawled out over me, fast asleep.

I didn't want to wake her.

Ugh, it sucked balls that she was still so ill. All I wanted to do was wake her up and tell her how I felt. Better yet, I could *show* her just how much I loved her.

I sighed.

All that would have to wait until she felt better. She needed rest, and I wasn't about to interrupt her sleep.

When I glanced over at the nightstand by the bed, where my phone was charging, I noticed there was a text notification.

Huh.

Carefully, I extricated myself from under Maisie, laying her back down gently on the pillows.

Then I grabbed my phone.

The text was from one of my Team USA teammates, Blake Cavaletti. After the championships had ended, he'd changed his original plans to go back to New York, and had instead embarked on a tour of Europe.

Apparently, he was back in Stockholm, preparing to fly back over to the States now. That was what he wrote in his first text.

There was another from him too, and that one read: **Guess who just got traded to the Las Vegas Wolves? Yep, yours truly did.**

I ran my hand down my face, grinning. This was awesome news.

I'd been hoping that the team would pick up Blake. He was a talented right winger, and a great addition to the Wolves organization.

He'd sent the messages not that long ago, so I texted him back.

Me: **I can't believe it, man. I am so amped. You're going to love playing for the Wolves.**

My phone dinged within seconds.

Blake: **I'm looking forward to it.**

Me: **Me too. Who did they trade for you?**

Blake: **Some dude named Drew Chidders.**

Me: **Ugh. He's a douche. Good riddance.**

Blake went on to tell me his flight was later tonight.

And then he wrote: **Would you want to meet up for a quick drink before I head to the airport? I'm at the hotel right now. We can celebrate my coming to the Wolves and talk more in person.**

I looked over at Maisie, sleeping soundly. I then felt her forehead. Her fever appeared to have broken.

Good.

I didn't see any harm in leaving for a short while, so I told Blake that yes, I'd meet him downstairs.

A short while later, he and I were in the hotel bar, the same place where I'd first laid eyes on Maisie. Thank God the bartender from that night wasn't working. I didn't feel like dealing with his death stares. Blake and I were having too much of a good time for that bullshit.

We were talking about the Wolves, Las Vegas, and the upcoming season.

"Yeah," Blake said, "once I'm back in New York, I'll start preparing for my move."

I assured him, "You're going to love Vegas, man. The guys on the team are great. We have such a good time out there."

"I bet," he replied. "I'm really looking forward to this season."

Blake was clearly excited to join the team, which was great. Enthusiastic players like him were what led to championship seasons.

After taking a long pull from my bottled beer, I said, "Do you think you'll be moved in by training camp?"

He nodded. "Yeah, I'm sure of it. I'd like to get settled as soon as possible. I'm not much of a procrastinator."

"Cool."

Blake told me he was also glad he already had a friend on the team, meaning me.

I said, "For sure."

We had so much catching up to do and things to plan for once he was in Vegas. We discussed all that and the next thing I knew, we'd been at the bar for a couple of hours.

"Fuck." Blake looked down at his watch. "I better get rolling, or I'm going to miss my flight."

"Shit, you're right. Go, go. I should check in on Maisie, anyway. We've been here for a long time."

"We have. At least three hours."

"Yeah."

I'd told Blake about the amazing woman I'd met in Stockholm. I had shown him pictures on my phone too, ones we'd taken when we were in Oslo.

"Wow, man, she is really fucking pretty," Blake had said.

I'd turned the phone back my way, smiling down at the image of the woman I loved, murmuring, "I know, right?"

Blake thought it had to have been fate that brought us together, seeing as we lived in neighboring states but probably would have never met.

Thank God for Stockholm.

I also had told Blake I'd fallen in love with Maisie, but had yet to tell her.

And that was the subject Blake returned to before he left.

Standing, he said, "Hey, about Maisie. Can I say one thing before I go?"

"Yeah, sure. What's up?"

He cleared his throat. And then he looked at me like I better damn well listen up.

Finally, he said, "You should definitely let Maisie know how you feel. It's never a good idea to wait on these kinds of things. Get it out there, Noel, show your hand. You just don't know when the moment could be lost."

Nodding, I agreed wholeheartedly, "Yeah, you're right. I plan to tell her real soon."

Blake was insistent, though, his dark brown eyes somber.

"No, seriously, dude. There is no time like the fucking present. Tell her how much you care about her as soon as you're back up in that room."

He had a point.

Why put it off?

Blowing out a breath, I said, "You're absolutely right. I'm on it, don't worry. As soon as I see her, I'm going to tell Maisie that I love her."

He patted me on the shoulder. "Good, man."

Well, it was official.

Tonight would be the night I'd profess my love to Maisie Troy.

PLANS ALTERED

MAISIE

woke up feeling much better. My fever was gone, and I had some actual energy.

This is great!

I got up out of bed and stretched, glancing around the room.

Noel wasn't there, so I assumed he'd gone out to wrangle us up some dinner. He had to have been as tired of room service as I was. I sure had bitched about it enough before getting sick.

I felt so good and refreshed that I wanted to freshen up, so I made my way to the bathroom.

After shedding my pajamas onto the cool tile floor, I jumped in the tub, enjoying a long, hot shower. I felt so good I even washed my hair…twice.

Only problem was after I got out and toweled off, I realized the only clothes I had in Noel's room were the jeans and long-sleeved tee I'd had on yesterday.

And those were gross.

I looked down at the discarded garments, draped over a hamper. No way was I putting "sick clothes" back on for the whole rest of the day.

I would have to go up to my room and retrieve some fresh clothing.

After I slipped on panties and a bra, which I also planned to swap out, I unfortunately had to don the tee and jeans for the time being, along with my beat-up Chucks.

I thought about leaving a short note for Noel, informing him of where I was going, but I wasn't going to be gone long enough to warrant it. I'd probably make it back to the room before him.

Grabbing the key card, I left.

The elevator was slow, and it felt like forever before I reached my floor.

Finally, I was making my way down the long hall to my suite.

But at the door, before I even waved the key card in front of the lock, something felt off.

I couldn't put my finger on what it was, though, that was bothering me.

Only once I stepped into the room, and the door had closed behind me, did it hit me.

Holy shit! I hadn't needed to use my key card!

The door had been ever-so-slightly ajar.

How had I not noticed something so major?

I was clearly still not myself.

But I did realize one thing—I needed to turn around and haul my ass out of there.

Last thing I wanted was to come face-to-face with an intruder, not in my weakened condition.

Squeezing my eyes shut and gritting my teeth—hoping too I had not been discovered—I spun around, ready to make a run for the door.

But before I took a single step, someone emerged from the bathroom.

I froze, and then a deep male rang out, "Maisie? Maisie Troy? Is that you?"

I stayed frozen.

Yikes.

He'd said my name.

This was someone who knew me.

But who knew me in Stockholm?

Only Noel.

And it wasn't his voice I'd heard.

I started freaking out, keeping cool on the outside, though.

Opening my eyes, I slowly reached for the doorknob. Maybe I could still sneak out of here.

Too late.

Someone placed a hand over mine.

Help!

"Not so fast there," the strange male said. "I'm not going to hurt you, but we need to talk."

He moved his hand away from mine, telling me, "Turn around and face me."

I'm trapped.

Slowly, I turned around, backing up as I did, and only stopping once I could slump against the door.

I needed it for support or I would pass out.

Before me stood a tall man in a black suit, about thirty, with dark blond hair and icy blue eyes.

His cold stare gave me a chill.

Or maybe it was my illness causing that.

"I'm Robert," he said all formally. "I'm Gary's accountant."

It all fell into place then, and I murmured a shaky, "Oh, fuck."

He smiled smugly. "Fuck is right, Ms. Troy."

I was so busted.

"Uh, I guess you discovered the charges on the room and realized the Juice King wasn't here."

"Among other things," he replied.

A curious response, so I asked, "What other things?"

"Let's just say your mother finally decided to share with my client that you've been utilizing his suite for quite some time."

Pressing back into the door as much as I could, wishing I could just disappear to the other side, I squeaked out, "Has it really been all that long?"

"It's been a couple of months, yes."

Had I been in Sweden that long?

Noel made the time go so fast.

Noel…

He was going to find out everything about me now, all my secrets. And he'd probably end up hating me.

Ugh, I should've told him when I had the chance. Coming clean once you're busted doesn't carry too much weight.

I was sure Noel would see it that way too.

"I am so, so fucked," I mumbled, choking up.

"Yes, you are, Ms. Troy." Robert chuckled like he was enjoying this far too much. "You owe my client quite a bit of money."

"Wait, what?" I was stunned. "You do realize there's no way I can ever pay him back."

"We don't expect you to," he said.

I breathed a sigh of relief. "Thank God."

"Not so fast there."

Robert narrowed his cold eyes at me.

I didn't think he liked me very much.

"What we do expect you to do," he continued, his voice hardening, "is to pack up your shit and get the fuck out of here. We don't want you ever coming back."

He was scaring me, and I nodded profusely.

"Okay, I can do that. But can I talk to someone first?"

He barked out a humorless laugh. "If you mean speak with that guy you've been fucking, the answer is no. We want you gone from the premises as soon as possible. In fact, I'll help you gather your things."

He spun around and walked over to the closet where my suitcase was stored.

How does he know so much?

He must've cased the place before I returned. Maybe he even followed me. That would explain how he knew about Noel.

But I wasn't just "fucking" Noel. I loved him.

And now he'd never know.

Grabbing my suitcase from the closet roughly, Robert tossed it out onto the floor, where it popped open.

In a purely business tone, he said, "Now get packing, Ms. Troy."

"B-but I have nowhere to go," I protested, not knowing if Noel would want me anywhere near him once he knew the truth.

Flatly, Robert said, "Don't worry about that. You're going home."

"Yeah, good luck with that." I laughed. "I have no money for a plane ticket. Why do you think I stayed in the first place?"

Robert slipped a piece of paper from his suit pocket and handed it over to me.

"Here," he said. "That's your flight info. My client bought you a one-way ticket to Las Vegas, Nevada. I have some pocket money for you too. I'm sure you can find your way home to Two Palms from there, right?"

"Do I have a choice?" I murmured.

"No."

I sighed, and he said, "I'm warning you, Ms. Troy. If you do not go straight to the airport, my client *will* press charges. We don't want you just gone from this room; we want you out of the country."

It was ironic. I'd wanted a plane ticket home for so long, so much so that I had duped Noel into caring for me.

But now that he did care for me *and* I had a ticket home, I didn't want to go.

I couldn't leave Noel.

But what choice did I have?

This man wasn't about to let me stay.

It was clear from his stance as he stood there looking at me disdainfully that he meant business. I had no doubt he'd call the police if I protested, or tried to outsmart him.

What would I do anyway?

Run to Noel for help?

Ha, he was about to be done with me, he just didn't know it yet.

He would find out the truth soon enough, though. And he'd know I wasn't who he thought I was.

Clearing my throat, I asked Robert, "Is it okay if I write a note? We could pin it on the outside of the door."

He surprisingly agreed. "Sure, I don't see why not."

Before he changed his mind—or I did—I hastily penned my goodbye.

> Noel,
> I hate having to hurt you, but Ive come to realize we can never be.
> See, Im not who you think I am. I never was. All this time, Ive just been an illusion.
> Thats why I have to go now.
> Please know that Im sorry for everything.
> But mostly, Im sorry I hurt you.
> Maisie

After Noel discovered our whole relationship was built on lies, he'd never want to see or talk to me ever again. I was sure of it.

That thought made me want to cry.

And tears did fill my eyes as I taped the note to the outside of the door, hoping no one would bother it.

I then began to gather my things.

Robert, making good on his promise, helped me pack.

As he handed me a makeup bag he retrieved from the bathroom, he said, "You're actually lucky my client was kind enough to buy you passage home."

Swiping away a tear, I replied, "Yeah, why's that? My mom is dating him, after all. I highly doubt he'd make her mad by leaving me stranded out on the street."

"They're not dating anymore," Robert informed me. "They broke up a couple of weeks ago."

"What?" I gasped. "My mom never thought to call and tell me this?"

He shrugged, and I asked, "Or are you saying she just now told your client I was here?"

"I'm afraid, yes, that's what occurred," he replied. "Your mother and my client spoke on the phone recently. She fessed up then."

Another dagger reamed through my heart. I couldn't believe I had such a thoughtless mother.

But it was par for the course.

"Where is she now?" I asked. "My mother, that is."

Robert shrugged. "In Two Palms, I assume. That is your home, yes?"

"Not anymore," I muttered, but softly so Robert wouldn't hear.

One thing was now certain—armed with this update, there was no way in hell I was ever going back to Arizona.

I also planned to make sure no one could ever find me.

SHE'S GONE

NOEL

Before I went back to my hotel room, I picked up some food from a street vendor outside the hotel.

Maisie had to be hungry, right?

Chicken broth could only take you so far, and I knew how much she loved those open-faced shrimp and cucumber sandwiches.

But when I went upstairs with the bag containing our dinner, Maisie wasn't in the room.

"That's weird," I said as I set the bag of wrapped sandwiches down on the dresser. "Maybe she went up to her room to grab some clean clothes?"

After checking the bathroom, where her pajamas lay strewn out on the floor, I felt sure that she'd definitely gone to her room to get fresh clothes. Based on not just the discarded sleepwear, but the damp towel as well, I also surmised she had taken a shower.

Fantastic.

Maisie was feeling better.

I was pumped, thinking how she'd be back any minute. We could talk; I could tell her I loved her. Ah, life was good.

Whistling, I cleared off the little table by the window and took our sandwiches out of the bag.

We had water in the mini-fridge, so I grabbed two bottles.

And then I finally took a seat at the tiny table.

Time ticked by, but no Maisie.

Fifteen minutes passed, then thirty.

Next thing I knew it'd been over an hour, and still, Maisie had not come back.

This is weird.

"What could be taking her so long?" I wondered out loud as I ran my hand down my face. "I guess she could have fallen asleep in her room, right?"

Or maybe she just didn't have the energy to come back down.

The thought of Maisie in distress was unacceptable.

"That's it." I jumped up. "I better go see what's going on."

On the elevator ride up to her floor, I had this weird, overwhelmingly bad feeling.

Shit, I hope Maisie didn't have a relapse.

If that were the case, I'd just have to stay up in her room with her.

Damn, I was feeling even more off by the time I reached her floor and stepped out of the elevator.

It was eerie in the hall too, which didn't help matters. Everything was so quiet, not a person in sight.

As I started down the hall, I noticed a piece of paper was taped to the door to Maisie's suite.

What the…?

I picked up the pace, walking faster.

And then I started jogging when I saw the paper contained a handwritten note of some sort.

"That looks like Maisie's writing," I murmured as I reached the suite.

Ripping the note from the door, I read what was written on it.

God, I felt like I was punched in the gut.

"What the fuck?"

Maisie was gone?

Where did she go?

Back home?

It certainly sounded like it.

But what was up with this "we can never be" and "I'm just an illusion" crap?

Maisie was the most real person I knew. That was one of the reasons why I'd fallen in love with her.

Fuck, why hadn't I told her as much?

I glanced around.

Maybe she was still in the hotel?

Or maybe she was hiding in her room?

I had to find out, but when I tried the handle, the door was locked.

Shit.

I searched the floor for someone, anyone, who could help.

I eventually found a hotel employee, a girl who looked to be in her early twenties.

Good, I could work with that.

It took some cajoling, and a lot of flirting, but I finally talked her into opening the door to Maisie's room for me.

As soon as I walked in, I knew she was really gone. All of her things were missing, and the room just had an empty feel to it.

The employee had a tablet device, so I asked, "Can you check to see if the occupant is checked out?"

She was hesitant at first, but when she saw how upset I was I think she took pity on me.

"Okay," she acquiesced. "I'll check for you."

"Thanks," I replied. "I really appreciate it."

The girl tapped on her tablet for a few seconds, but then suddenly stopped.

"What is it?" I asked, heart hammering.

Staring down at the screen, she said, "It's just that something is very odd."

"What's odd?" I asked.

Looking up at me, she said, "It says here this room is still rented out, but not by a girl."

Huh?

"What?"

"Yes, look. See here…" She turned the screen to me, and I could see a bunch of charges for food and such, but they were all listed under the name of some dude named Gary Tarrington.

"Who the hell is that?" I bellowed.

The girl shrugged. "I don't know, sir. I'm new here. But he appears to have this suite rented for the rest of the year."

I let out a surprised, "Huh? What are you saying? That this guy rents this suite for the whole year? The dude must be loaded. More importantly, though, who the fuck is he to Maisie?"

The employee had no clue, of course, and neither did I.

But I sure as hell intended to find out.

VEGAS, BABY

MAISIE

touched down in Las Vegas early the next day.

Robert, as promised, had given me a few hundred dollars in US currency so I could make my way home to Two Palms.

Yeah, right.

I had no intention of ever going back to Arizona. That's where my jilted mother was. And after all her betrayals, she was the last person I cared to see.

I decided instead to use the cash to rent a cheap motel room in Vegas. I figured I'd just stay there till the money ran out.

Or maybe I can get a job and stick around for as long as I like.

That sounded like a better plan.

So over the next few days, I applied at a bunch of different places. Thanks to my cashier experience from back in Two Palms, a small convenience store hired me right away.

It sucked a little, as it was kind of far from my crummy motel.

But just as I'd done when I put in the application, I'd simply take the bus.

Maybe it was for the best. I'd be working in a safer part of town. The convenience store was right where the bus line ended, and a fancy new suburb of freshly constructed homes was located just around the block.

It would be like it always was for me—I'd be on the outside, looking into a life I'd never have.

You were so close, Maisie.

Too bad I'd blown it.

Lies, deception… Noel was probably happy to be rid of me.

Too bad I still loved him and missed him like crazy.

"I can cover any shift you need," I told my new manager.

I planned to work as much as I could. Not just for the money, but to help me forget about Noel. Hopefully it would work.

Unfortunately, it didn't.

As the first couple of weeks of my new employment dragged on, I still felt sad and lonely. I missed Noel every second of every day. I knew I should try to make connections, find some friends.

But I couldn't.

My heart just wasn't in it. It ached far too much.

The people at work were nice, but I kept my distance, leading my life of solitude.

That was fine. I deserved nothing more.

My new existence consisted of taking the bus to work, putting in my hours, and returning to my motel room, where I slept and sometimes watched TV.

The only thing I allowed myself that was in any way reminiscent of how I'd lived my summer in Sweden, was to learn everything I could about hockey.

It was my last and only connection to Noel, and I could feel close to him without the possibility of hurting him again.

My mom, surprisingly, was still paying my cell phone bill, so I had an internet connection. And Google was my friend. All my searches were hockey related, and I began to learn a lot more about the sport.

It pleased me to think how, if things were still good with us, Noel would have been so impressed.

Too bad he'd never know.

Besides my own commitment to stay away from him, he'd already given up on me.

I knew that because the first week or so after I'd left Sweden, he left tons of voice mails and texts.

But then he'd stopped.

No matter, it was for the best. That was why I deleted each and every one of his messages, never listening or reading a single one.

What would be the point?

The content was most likely about how much I'd hurt him, and how he totally hated me.

I couldn't take that.

Of course, even though his efforts to contact me had ceased, my interest in him hadn't waned. It was like I *needed* to know what Noel and the Las Vegas Wolves were up to.

So I kept up my research.

The regular season was only a few weeks away, and training camp was nearing. Some of the guys were already streaming back into town, including Noel.

My heart!

There was a huge interview with him that had been published on some hockey blog.

I ate that up.

Most of the questions were hockey-related, but there was one about his love life.

When I greedily read what he had to say, my soul was crushed. I knew for sure that he'd moved on.

Interviewer: Tell us, Noel. Is there a special lady in your life these days?

Noel: Uh, there was someone I met in Sweden. Let's just say, though, that it didn't work out.

Interviewer: So you're telling us that you're available?

Noel (laughing): Yes, I guess you could say that.

Interviewer: Single and ready to mingle, huh?

Noel: I suppose.

Even though my heart was broken, I knew it was for the best.

Noel Sandlund was better off without me.

26

BUMFUCK NOWHERE

NOEL

Before I left Sweden, and after I arrived back in Las Vegas, I left Maisie a ton of messages.

Voice mails, texts, all with me pleading for her to please get back to me and tell me why she had left in such a rush.

Whatever made her run could be fixed, right?

I mean, I loved her, damn it.

And love could fix anything, even misunderstandings or misrepresentations of oneself.

That's right. I didn't buy any of the things she'd written in her note, especially not the "illusion" crap.

I didn't care what she thought. I knew the real Maisie, and I knew what was in her heart.

That was why I *had* to find her.

I left Stockholm the day after I found her note, and then I spent the next week or so messaging her.

When I received no responses, I decided to quit.

Trying to reach Maisie electronically just wasn't working.

I was in no way done, though.

On the contrary, I knew it was simply time to take the bull by the horns. And by that I meant I was taking a trip to good ole Two Palms, Arizona.

Maisie Troy was not getting away from me that easily. I was one determined motherfucker when I needed to be.

That was how I had discovered who Gary Tarrington was—a fifty-something dude who owned a huge juice company.

There was no way in hell Maisie had any interest in him.

First, she wouldn't have been able to keep him hidden from me in Sweden. I was in her hotel suite way too many times, and there was never a hint of any dude staying there.

Then there was the fact that Maisie didn't even like juice all that much.

No way was she humping a Juice King.

But still, the question of how she had ended up in his room in the first place lingered.

I thought about it for hours.

What I eventually came up with was that maybe the friend she'd been traveling with had hooked up with this Gary guy.

Yeah, that was plausible.

Hadn't Maisie mentioned the night I met her that her friend had taken off with some dude?

Yes, yes she had.

That had to be why she'd had the suite all to herself.

It was starting to all make sense.

It was also probably why Maisie wrote in her note that she was just an illusion, because the suite wasn't really her room.

Didn't she realize I didn't care about crap like that?

Why she'd even think such a thing would bother me, I had no clue.

I'd have to ask her once I got to Two Palms.

Speaking of which, I was almost there.

I started out this morning, and it was now near noon. I'd already crossed the state line and exited the highway, but I was beginning to wonder if maybe my GPS wasn't working.

I'd been driving in desolate desert for quite some time, with no civilization in sight.

I hit Recalibrate, but the GPS assured me I was traveling in the right direction.

"Okay then, let's do this."

GPS was right.

I soon saw signs for Two Palms, popping up along the side of the road, looking like lonely sentinels in the arid, barren landscape.

"Maisie sure lives in bumfuck nowhere," I muttered.

I was going pretty fast, but I had to slow down to swerve and avoid a lizard sunning itself in the middle of the road.

"Yeesh, it really is no-man's-land out here," I lamented as I watched the little guy scurry off in my rearview mirror.

My eyes returned to the road and up in the distance, finally, a tiny town came into view.

Small would have been an understatement in describing Two Palms.

There was one good thing about that, though.

In a town that tiny, there was no place Maisie Troy could hide.

27

DAMN WOLVES ARE EVERYWHERE

MAISIE

It was nearing evening, and my shift was done in an hour.

Thank God.

It'd been an especially trying day, and I couldn't wait to grab the bus and return to the motel.

Noel had been on my mind more than usual, which was really saying something since I pretty much thought of him all the time.

Some days were like that—twenty-four hours of constant reminders of Noel.

Things got even worse when a new employee at the store, a young girl around my age named Fiona, wouldn't stop going on and on about hockey, specifically the Wolves.

She wanted to talk about the players, the team, and the upcoming season.

Figures, I'd be stuck working with the Wolves' biggest fan.

As we stood there at the register in the front of the store, during an unfortunately quiet lull, she said, "Oh, Maisie, I really hope they keep Dylan Culderway and Noel Sandlund together. It's been weighing on my mind like you wouldn't believe."

"It has?" I queried.

"Yes. They're one of the best defensive pairings in the league. You must know that, Maisie. You live here, right?"

"Right," I glumly replied.

Ugh.

It hurt to hear Noel's name. But I had to play dumb to end this discussion. Otherwise, I'd tear up and that would look really weird. Fiona would wonder why hockey talk made me cry.

So, clearing my throat, I said, "No, I wasn't aware of that. But thanks for the update."

I thought the conversation was dead right there.

But no, it took a turn for the worst.

"Which one do you think is the hottest?" Fiona asked as she toyed with one of her auburn braids.

"I told you I don't follow hockey," I snapped.

My attitude didn't deter her in the slightest.

"That's not a problem," she said, whipping out her phone and tapping on the screen.

To my horror, she then turned it my way.

"Here are headshots of all the players," she said. "They're on the team website. That's pretty convenient, huh?"

"Er…"

"So which one do you prefer, Maisie? Noel or Dylan?"

Of course she flipped right past Dylan's pic and stopped on Noel's.

It was clear who her favorite was—my freaking man!

Or, at least, he used to be.

Wearily, I stared at Noel's face on the screen. It was such a good picture of him, capturing not only how handsome he was, but also his kind demeanor.

He looked so freaking happy in the shot too, kind of how he once looked with me before I ruined everything.

I better answer her question.

I didn't want to open my mouth just yet, though. Fiona would wonder why my voice was cracking. It would too, seeing as pesky tears were already blurring my vision.

Too late, you're busted.

"Hey, are you okay?" Fiona lowered her phone.

I swished my hand in front of my face, like that would make it all go away.

Too bad it didn't work.

"Yes, yes, I'm fine," I blathered. "There's something in my eye, I think."

Thank God Fiona believed me.

"Oh, that's not good." She frowned. "Why don't you go back to the bathroom and fix it? I'll cover for you."

I was thinking of taking her up on her offer, simply to get away, but then the door jingled open and a customer walked in.

The next thing I knew, and before I had a chance to turn around, Fiona grabbed my arm and exclaimed under her breath, "Oh my God, Maisie! There's one of them now. I can't freaking believe it. A Wolves player just strolled into our store!"

Say what?

No!

I wasn't about to turn around and look, because what if...?

"Which player is it?" I asked shakily.

Please don't be Noel. Please don't be Noel.

To my relief, Fiona said, "It's the new guy, Blake Cavaletti."

"Oh, thank heavens." I blew out a breath.

"Here he comes, Maisie." Fiona shook me. "You can't leave me. In fact, you have to wait on him. I'm too nervous, and I don't want to make a fool of myself."

I had no choice, not really, so I muttered a flat, dead-sounding, "Sure, whatever."

There was no harm in waiting on this Blake dude. I'd never met him, and he had no clue who I was, or that I knew Noel.

When I heard him step up to the counter, I spun around to face him.

Fiona just kind of hung behind me, drooling.

I knew that because when I ventured a glance back, she was staring at Blake all dreamy-eyed.

Oh, Lord.

I pivoted back to Blake. There was no denying he was an extremely good-looking guy. Italian features, with slicked-back black hair, deep brown eyes, and bronzed skin.

Hmm...

Sexy and hot were words that came to mind.

Still, he had no effect on me. I only had eyes for Noel, even if we weren't together.

Flashing me a sexy grin, Blake placed a big energy drink on the counter.

"Is that all?" I asked, ringing it up.

"Yep, that's it," he replied.

And that's when, for no reason I could discern, things got really weird.

Blake narrowed his eyes at me. Not in any kind of bad way. No, this was more like he was trying to place me or something.

But that couldn't be right. There was no way in hell he knew who I was.

Yeah, I probably just looked like someone from his past.

Giving it no further thought, I said, "That'll be $4.75, please."

Blake handed me his credit card.

I swiped it, then said, "Thanks. Have a nice evening."

I handed him his receipt, and his eyes held mine intently.

When I frowned, he looked away. "Yeah, you too, miss."

After he left, Fiona grabbed me by the arm.

"Maisie, Maisie, holy hell. Blake Cavaletti was looking at you like he totally knew you. Have you met him before?"

I shook my head. "No, never."

"Ooh," she trilled, "maybe he likes you, then?"

"I don't think that was it."

"Then what was it?" Fiona pressed.

I shrugged and replied honestly, "I have no idea."

I was a little worried, though. There was no denying there'd been recognition in Blake's steady gaze.

But that's impossible.

Yeah, I just wasn't feeling myself today.

I was reading too much into it.

There was no way in hell Blake Cavaletti knew I was the girl who broke his teammate's heart.

28

HOLY F*CKING SHIT

NOEL

F inding Maisie's trailer wasn't difficult at all.

The first gas station I stopped at, which appeared to be the *only* gas station in town, I found an old grizzled male attendant who knew exactly where the Troys lived.

"Ah, yes, sonny," he said, pointing westward. "Just follow the main road down a spell, and take the third street on your left. Follow that to the end. You'll come right up on the Troys' trailer."

He was right.

Following his directions, I was at my destination.

I looked at Maisie's home, the trailer long and squat and a light blue color. Not a light blue like it'd been painted that way, but more a faded, sun-bleached version of what it once was.

I sighed, making my way to the front door.

I knocked for a solid minute, until finally a pretty woman in her forties appeared.

I was stunned. This woman was an older version of Maisie, though a little rough around the edges.

I knew right away she had to be Maisie's mom.

What I didn't expect was for the woman to lean on the doorframe and blatantly start flirting with me.

"Oh, honey," she purred, sizing me up with a thorough once-over. "Who, pray tell, are you? And what brings you all the way out here? Are you lost or something? If you are, I can definitely help."

She batted her long, dark lashes at me.

Though she was definitely attractive, I wasn't about to lead Maisie's mom on.

Giving her a withering look—like are-you-for-real-lady?—I replied, "No, I'm not lost. I'm actually looking for you."

Encouraged, she trilled, "You are, are you?"

She jutted her chest out, her clingy, cleavage-bearing blouse almost busting at the seams.

I ignored her, uh…assets.

"I don't mean what I think you're thinking," I scoffed.

Annoyed her ploy wasn't working, her whole demeanor changed.

"What do you want, then?" she snapped. "If you're selling something, mister, I'm not interested. As you can see"—she waved her hand at the run-down trailer—"I'm not exactly rolling in dough out here."

"Don't worry," I assured her. "I'm not selling anything. My name is Noel, Noel Sandlund. And I'm looking for who I think may be your daughter. Her name is Maisie Troy."

"Oh, her…" Maisie's mom, to my utter shock and surprise, rolled her eyes.

"She kind of means a lot to me," I went on, "and we've sort of lost touch."

The woman took no pity on me, stating matter-of-factly, "Maisie is my daughter, yes, but you're out of luck. I have no idea where the ungrateful bitch could be. I'll tell you one thing, though. She should be back here helping me pay the goddamn bills. She's lucky I haven't cut off her cell service yet. I will soon. I'm just getting such a good deal with two lines instead of one." She waved her hand. "But that's neither here nor there. Her habit of freeloading is getting old. My daughter has no appreciation for anything I do for her. I mean, she spends practically the whole summer in my ex-boyfriend's hotel room, in fucking Sweden, no less, never paying a dime, and still—"

"Wait, what?" I had to interrupt. I'd had enough of her bitching, anyway. "Are you saying the juice guy, Gary, is *your* boyfriend?"

"Yes," she snorted indignantly. "I mean, he was. But he will be again if *I* have anything to say about it."

Whoa.

Here I'd been thinking this whole time that Maisie's "friend" and traveling companion was a girl her age, not her freaking *mother*.

Poor Maisie.

I suddenly understood a lot more about her situation. It made so much more sense too why she'd taken off abruptly. And why she hadn't talked to me in the first place to explain the situation.

Maisie had been embarrassed, and probably feeling bad she'd withheld the real details of her life from me.

I wouldn't have cared or been bothered.

Hell, I was fine with all this now.

I loved Maisie, and just as I'd maintained from the start, stupid shit didn't matter.

"Ma'am," I began. "Do you have any idea at all where Maisie could be?"

Shaking her head, she replied, "No. I'm sorry, but I really don't. If you find her, though, tell her I don't plan on staying in Two Palms much longer."

"Why's that?"

Rolling back her shoulders, she sniffed. "I told you, I'm working on getting back with Gary. And when he finally sees the light, which he will, I am out of here."

Appalled, I retorted, "What if Maisie comes home and you're gone?"

Shit, I really needed to find her. I wasn't about to let the woman I loved end up truly homeless.

Her mother shrugged. "I don't know. But I'm sure she'll land on her feet."

I couldn't take much more of her callousness, so I muttered a sarcastic, "Well, thanks for your time. You've been a real help."

I turned to leave, but she stopped me.

"Hey, wait. Hold on a minute. I have some things for you to give Maisie if you do find her."

I turned around, and she held up a red talon-nailed finger.

Then she disappeared.

I stood there waiting for about five minutes.

When she reappeared, she shoved a black garbage bag full of what looked like clothes into my arms. And then she plopped a floppy-eared stuffed dog atop the bag.

"That's all of Maisie's stuff," she said, wiping her hands down the sides of her tight jeans. "I really don't think she's coming back anytime soon. And like I told you, I don't plan on sticking around. So if you find her"—her tone softened a bit—"tell her those are the rest of her clothes, and the only thing that's ever meant anything to her."

I readjusted the bag under my arm so I could hold up the stuffed animal.

"Do you mean this dog?"

Maisie's mom nodded. "Uh-huh, yeah. That old thing was the last gift her father ever gave her, before the no-good bastard took off for good."

The stuffed animal looked old and worn, so I assumed Maisie's dad had left a really long time ago.

With a curt nod, I promised I'd make sure Maisie got her things.

As if I didn't have reason enough already, I absolutely had to find her now.

But how?

Where in the hell was she?

By the time I was back in my car, I was sick with worry. One of the worst feelings in the world is not having any idea where someone you love is.

As I drove away from the trailer Maisie once called home, the last of her worldly possessions in my care, my cell phone rang.

When I looked on the display panel, I saw that it was Blake.

I hit a button on the steering wheel to answer his call. I'd heard he bought a house in the suburbs of Vegas and had recently moved in. We hadn't had a chance to talk since Sweden, and since I had a long drive ahead of me, I figured it'd be a good opportunity to catch up.

Not to mention, I needed to get Maisie off my mind. I had to concentrate on driving.

The call connecting, I said, "Hey, man."

"Hey, Noel," Blake replied, sounding kind of serious.

"It's good to hear from you," I went on. "I've been meaning to touch base."

"Yeah, me too, me too." He sighed. "Things have been crazy lately with settling in and all."

"Yeah, I bet," I said.

"Anyway, so..."

Blake sounded odd, like there was another reason for his call besides getting caught up.

So I just asked, "What's really up?"

He cleared his throat. "Uh, maybe something, I'm not sure. But first I have a question for you."

I had no idea where this was going.

But I replied, "Go ahead, shoot."

"Remember that girl you told me about when we were in Sweden? You showed me some pictures of her that you had on your phone."

Shit, of course I remembered. But what could this be about?

Hesitantly, I said, "Yeah. What about her?"

My pulse raced, and I clutched the wheel so tightly my knuckles turned white.

Carefully, Blake said, "First, I have another question."

"All right..."

"Did you ever tell her that you loved her, like you said you were going to?"

Okay, this was getting weird.

"No. Why do you ask?"

"It's just," he sighed. "You're never going to believe this, but I swear I saw that same girl working in a convenience store here in Las Vegas."

I jerked the wheel, yanking the car off to the side of the road. Dust flew up everywhere.

"Holy fuck!" I exclaimed. "What did you just say?"

He told me again.

It had to be Maisie.

So I asked for the address of the store.

Blake read it off from his receipt, and I entered the info into my GPS so fast it wasn't even funny.

We ended the call.

And then I was off and on my way to one fucking important-as-hell convenience store in Las Vegas.

29

HATE TO LOVE

MAISIE

As the minutes ticked down to the end of my shift, I grew more and more impatient.

What if that hockey player, Blake, had recognized me?

Noel and I had taken a lot of pictures together, both with his phone and mine. What if Noel had shown him even just one of his shots? Let alone a bunch of them.

Shit, I have to get out of here.

I had ten minutes left, but I asked Fiona if she could cover for me.

Peering at me curiously, she said, "Why? Are you not feeling well? Your eye's not still bothering you, is it?"

I shrugged. "No, but I think I may be getting sick."

It wasn't a lie.

I did feel ill, my heart was aching.

"Hmm, you do look a little flushed, Maisie."

I nodded. "Yeah, something's not right."

"Then go." She motioned to the door. "Don't worry. I got your back."

I smiled at her. "Thanks, Fiona."

"Not a problem."

The new girl was turning out to be nice, even if she was fixated on hockey. I was still glad to have her as a coworker.

After grabbing my purse from the back storeroom, I got the hell out of the store.

The bus stop was only a block away, and I rushed off to it.

It wasn't busy out on the street, which really sucked because I would have liked to have blended in. But, nope. This raven-haired girl in skinny jeans and a regulation navy blue Quik-Stop polo shirt stood out like a sore thumb.

I wasn't even surprised when I heard the low hum of an expensive sports car pull up to the curb along the sidewalk.

Hadn't I expected this all along?

I tried to look away as the car trailed me, but there was no use. There was no getting away.

Sure enough, a man called out, "Maisie? Is that you? It really is, isn't it?"

Great, all my fears had just been confirmed. It was Noel.

That Blake guy must've somehow recognized me.

Shit.

I wanted to run, but I couldn't. Noel was in a car. He'd catch up easily. Not to mention, he'd jump out and chase me on foot if he had to.

Choking up, I stopped and turned to the idling car. It was a bright red, shiny Porsche Panamera, and Noel was in the driver's seat.

Seeing him tore me apart.

"Just leave me alone," I sobbed, since the passenger window was down and he could hear me. "I know you hate me. Why'd you come here, anyway? Do you want an apology? If so, here it is... I'm sorry I left Sweden so quickly and without more than a note. I had no choice, not really. But whatever." I threw my hands up in the air. "All you need to know is that it was all for the best, Noel."

"Maisie, how can you say that?" he gasped.

Cutting the ignition, he got out of the car.

Again, I wanted to flee, but I couldn't make my sneakered feet move.

Damn it, my heart was screwing everything up.

"Maisie, please don't take off." Noel took a tentative step toward me. "Why don't you just get in the car for a minute so we don't have to talk out on the street?"

"What's it matter?" I cried. "There's no one around, anyway."

I was stalling. I knew I'd get in.

But Noel didn't know that, and he pleaded, "Please, Mais, I'm begging you."

I shook my head, but he was having none of it. Four long strides later and he'd reached me.

Taking my limp hand in his, he led me over to the passenger side of the car.

"Come on now," he murmured soothingly. "Just sit down for a sec. I think you'll be surprised at what I have to say."

I nodded, feeling numb.

By the time he had popped open the door, I was like a puppet on a string.

Noel helped me slip into his car, guiding me with his hand on my lower back.

Once I was inside, he closed the door and hurried over to the driver's side, where he jumped in so quickly it was almost funny. He was clearly afraid I'd come to my senses and make an escape.

I didn't want to escape, though. Not now. I didn't care if Noel had gotten me into his car so he could properly ream me out, I just wanted to, for one last time, be close to him.

Already, I bathed in his comforting, masculine scent.

Ahh...

It was soothing how the whole car smelled like leather and Noel. I felt heady and intoxicated; I never wanted to leave.

Like a fool drunk on the man who still owned her heart, I looked over and whispered, "Noel."

He smiled at me.

I was shocked. He didn't look angry at all.

How could that be?

I'd get to that, but I had some questions first.

"How'd you find me?" I croaked out. "Was it that Blake guy? Did he rat me out?"

"Yeah." Noel chuckled. "I showed him pictures of you and me together that time I met him when you were sick."

"I didn't know you met him out," I said. "But I figured it was something like that."

Quietly, Noel murmured, "I think it was fate, Maisie. Blake seeing you and all. Face it, babe"—he smiled over at me—"we're meant to be."

I squeaked, "Are you saying you don't hate me?"

He shook his beautiful head and laughed. "Are you kidding? I could never hate you."

"B-but I left you. And I have to be honest. I only pursued you in the beginning because I needed a plane ticket home. When I finally had one, I took off. I didn't even tell you why."

"Maisie," he sighed. "I don't care about all that. As far as I'm concerned, it's behind us. Besides, I know why you left."

My eyes widened. "You do?"

"Yes. And it's okay. I understand."

I blinked over at him, stunned. "How in the world could you know why I left?"

He reached for something in the back on the floor behind his seat.

When he pulled that something forward, he shocked me as he said, "I know because I've been to Two Palms. I was there today, right before I drove here. Maisie, I talked with your mom. I know all about what happened in Sweden."

I was barely listening, as I was focused on something I thought I'd never see again.

"Oh my God, Noel, you brought me Claude!"

He laughed as he handed me my old, beat-up stuffed dog.

"I did," he said. "And I also have some clothes for you in the back. Your mom gave me a bag of your things."

I rolled my eyes. "Of course she did. Let me guess? She's getting back with the Juice King."

He nodded. "She's trying."

"Great. Now she'll move away and I really won't have a home."

Noel went to reach for me, but hesitated.

I was sure it was because I looked a little crazy. This was just too much.

Softly, like how one would speak so as not to startle a scared animal, he said, "That's not true, Maisie. You're not homeless. I'd never let that happen to you."

I lost it then.

"Why would you even care?" I cried out.

I was holding onto Claude, choking back tears, when he finally leaned over and took me in his arms.

"Aw, fuck it." I heard him say.

"Noel," I sputtered. "I-I I just…"

"Maisie, Maisie," he soothed. "You don't have to say anything. Just let me speak, okay?"

"Okay."

"You keep repeating that I shouldn't care. And that I must hate you. But you are so wrong, so very, very wrong."

He caressed my hair, but stopped when I pulled back and looked up at him.

"You really don't hate me?" I asked.

My father leaving, the way my mother was—I was accustomed to people walking away. It was hard to fathom Noel could be any different.

But different he was.

He proved as much when he said, "I told you that I don't hate you. And I don't. I'll say it a thousand times if I have to." He took my face in his hands. "Fuck, Maisie, how haven't you figured it out yet?"

"Figured what out?" I asked.

"That I love you, you beautiful, complicated girl."

30

NOTHING HAS CHANGED

NOEL

I had told Maisie that I loved her.

And it was okay, because it was true.

As far as I could see, there'd never be a more perfect time to finally put it all out there, to lay my heart on the line.

"You do?" she whispered. "You really love me?"

Her face was still in my hands, so I leaned forward and kissed her lips lightly.

"Yes." I sat back and smiled. "I really do love you, sweetheart."

I wanted to hear her say it back to me, and it felt like she might, but I knew deep down she wasn't quite ready.

That was cool. I could wait.

It was clear I was going to have to be careful with Maisie's fragile heart. It'd been broken far too many times. Not by romantic interests, but by her own damn parents.

I kissed her soft lips once more.

Then, releasing her, I asked, "What are you thinking right now?"

She bit her lip. "I'm wondering if we can go somewhere more private."

"Sure. Where would you like to go?"

As I started the car, she said, "Is it all right if we go back to my motel room?"

"Motel room?"

"Yes, it's where I've been staying since I got back from Sweden."

I wanted to hear more details on how she'd gotten back, and what exactly went down, but those answers would come in time. For now I'd just do whatever she felt comfortable with.

So I asked her for directions, and we headed that way.

It didn't take long before we drove into a really crummy part of town.

I bit my tongue for a while, but when we pulled into the pitted parking lot of a seedy, run-down motel, I could no longer stay quiet.

"*This* is where you've been staying?" I exclaimed.

Lowering her head, she muttered a dejected, "Yes."

"Jesus, Maisie."

She chuckled bitterly. "I guess after seeing the trailer, and now this, your illusion of me is finally shattered."

She'd used those words in her note.

But she was wrong.

I tried to explain. "I'm not judging you, Maisie. Nothing about how I thought of you in Sweden has changed. Not one little bit. To me, you're still the same beautiful, witty, smart, perfect girl."

"Ha, not as carefree as you thought, though, right?"

I cocked my head and peered over at her. "I don't know about that. I think you've just had it a little rough lately. I know there's a carefree girl in there somewhere. Hell, I've seen her far too many times to doubt it."

She snorted, "Yeah, where?"

I ticked off, "At the park in Oslo, in Stockholm, and"—I lowered my voice—"in bed."

Swallowing hard, she looked over at me, her deep indigo eyes dark and mysterious in the dim glow of the barely lit parking lot.

Shocking the shit out of me, she suddenly said, "Take me there now then, Noel."

I was pretty sure I knew what she was saying, but I had to be sure. "What, to bed?"

She nodded and grabbed my hand. "Come."

Of course I was going. I wasn't ever letting her go again.

We released our linked hands just long enough to get out of the car. Then we were joined again.

I let Maisie lead me, just like she'd allowed me to help her into my car. Only this time we ended up in her motel room.

It wasn't as bad as I thought it would be. The room was tiny and the accommodations sparse, but the place was clean.

Not that I had much time to look around. Maisie was on me as soon as she closed the door.

"Noel…" She fumbled to unbutton the dress shirt I had on, yanking it from where it was tucked into my jeans.

I slid my hands up under her work shirt. "God, I've missed you so much."

Closing her eyes and standing on her tiptoes, her lips touched mine.

I let her kiss me her way—softly, cautiously.

And then I kissed her back my way—firmly, confidently.

Maisie melted into my arms, so I lifted her up and carried her over to the bed.

Laying her down on top of the covers, I undressed her like I was a kid at Christmas un-wrapping the best gift ever.

Maisie was exactly that.

She was perfection with her creamy white skin, pert rosy nipples, and the pink I longed for between her legs.

I let out a soft, wanting groan as I ditched my own clothes and kneeled on the floor.

"What are you doing?" she asked, lifting her head and peering down at me.

I spread her wide and responded, "This."

Once I tasted her nectar, it was like I couldn't get enough. She mewed and writhed until she fell apart.

Then she was still, except for the shaking.

Crawling up her body and settling between her quivering legs, I asked, "Are you all right?"

She nodded. "Uh-huh. I'm just happy. Jesus, it's been so long since I felt like this."

"Oh, Mais…" I kissed her. "I'm glad you feel good. I want you to be happy always."

I shifted so that my cock was where we both needed it to be.

But then I hesitated. I was concerned this was too much too soon.

Maisie was more than ready, though.

"Just do it, Noel," she rasped. "I want this. I *need* this. That's why I wanted to come back to the motel."

I didn't need any more encouragement than that. One quick thrust and I was sheathed inside her.

"Noel…"

Neither of us dared move. It felt good to just…be.

Pressing my forehead to hers, I said, "I know, sweetheart. I know."

Our union was perfect. It was coming home to where we both belonged—together, as one.

Eventually, though, the drive was too strong.

I had to move, and so did Maisie.

As I pumped into her, she met my every thrust.

I felt her building, building…then cresting and taking me with her.

As I emptied into Maisie, she cried out what I longed to hear, "I love you, Noel. I love you."

31

IT'S OUT THERE NOW

MAISIE

Shit, I had said the words.

In the throes of passion, I came clean.

So what did it mean?

Would Noel hurt me now that I'd bared my soul?

I closed my eyes and lay quietly beneath him, praying he wouldn't shatter my heart into a thousand pieces.

Noel, noticing how still I was, asked softly, "Maisie, what's wrong?"

I opened my eyes.

He appeared concerned.

He was probably thinking I regretted what I'd just said.

But I didn't, not at all.

I loved Noel Sandlund, more than I should have. And I believed he had a right to know.

Admitting it, though, caused me concern. I was terrified now. And I couldn't help it, but part of me wanted to run and hide.

I couldn't do that, certainly not when Noel was still on top of me and inside, partially hard.

There was no getting away.

I blinked up at him and confessed, "I'm just scared. That's all. I'm not used to baring my soul."

Kissing my forehead, he replied, "It's all right, Maisie. I want you to open up to me. I'm not going to hurt you."

I didn't know that for sure, so I begged, "Promise me that you won't."

"I promise, Maisie." He kissed me furiously. "I promise you with my life."

"I love you, Noel," I choked out between kisses.

"I love you too, sweet girl."

He swelled inside me, and we shifted together, groaning at how good it felt.

"Damn," I said.

"Right?" He nuzzled my neck. "I want you again. I swear I'll never get enough of you."

I slid along his shaft, and rasped, "Then have me, Noel. Feel how much I still want you. Take me."

Slipping his hands underneath me, he lifted me up and thrust into me.

"Yes," I cried out. "More, more!"

I couldn't get enough of him, either.

Noel, breathing hard and fast, rose to his knees and lifted my hips, working me along his cock.

"Oh, that feels *amazing*," I purred.

"Fuck, it does," he agreed.

Hitting my G-spot over and over with the new angle, I was left shaking and convulsing around his length, coming and begging, "Let go with me."

We cried out in pleasure together at the intensity of that moment.

Afterward, Noel lowered me down, collapsing on top of me.

"I love you, Mais," he murmured. "Fuck, it feels so good to say it out loud."

I was feeling more confident he wouldn't hurt me, just as he'd promised, so I stated resolutely, "I love you too."

Rolling onto his back, he smiled over at me.

Noel was clearly excited about something, so I snuggled into his warmth and asked, "What are you scheming over in that head of yours?"

"Oh, wouldn't you like to find out?"

"As a matter of fact, I would."

"Ah, I was just wondering what comes next for us."

"Hmm, we go to sleep?" I teased.

I was feeling good and lighthearted.

And so was Noel.

Laughing, he pulled me into his arms. "No way, Maisie girl. I'm not done with you yet."

"Mmm"—I hitched my leg over his hip—"so we're going for another round?"

"Yep. Just give me a few more minutes."

"Okay." I rested my chin on his chest. "You still haven't told me, though."

"Told you what?"

"What you meant by wondering what comes next for us?"

"Oh, that. I just meant in our relationship."

I was curious as to how he saw us moving forward, so I asked, "What do you see, Noel?"

He pondered, and said, "I see you and me together and happy, and with—" He grabbed my hand and kissed the back. "—a real future."

Even though I trusted Noel, and I wanted all those things badly, I regressed. Just like that, I was back to feeling scared as fuck.

Ugh.

I had a feeling this was how it was going to be for a while—a back-and-forth seesaw of emotion.

Healing just wasn't a straight-line event.

I didn't want to disappoint Noel. Sweden had been one thing. But it hadn't been real.

What if I couldn't be what he needed me to be here in Vegas?

This was the real world.

Would we make it?

I decided to open up and share all my fears with him.

When I finished, he said, "Look, I know you're afraid. But there's no reason to be. *You* are what I want and need, no matter if we're here, there, or anywhere. Trust me on that, all right?"

I murmured a shaky, "Okay."

Noel frowned. "That didn't sound convincing."

I sat up, blew out a breath.

"I'm trying here, Noel. I really am. But you can't expect me to feel fully confident that quickly."

Nodding, he agreed, "I know, Mais. And I don't expect that."

We needed to lighten things up, it was getting too heavy.

Groaning, I said, "Enough of that. I have another, more pressing question."

Raising a brow, he asked, "Oh, yeah? What's that?"

"I'm curious. What exactly do you plan on telling your friends and teammates when they ask how we met?"

He smiled mischievously. "I'm going to say I brought you back with me from Sweden."

"Noel, no!" I smacked his hard pec. "That makes it sound like I'm from there."

"Eh"—he shrugged—"so what if it does? They'll figure it out once they meet you. And, Maisie, trust me, my teammates are going to adore you." He reached up and caressed my cheek. "You'll fit right in with them *and* their girlfriends and wives."

I was glad he was so confident.

I wished I could feel the same.

Warily, I said, "I don't know about that."

The prospect of meeting all those talented athletes and their perfect women left me uneasy. But Noel was so pumped that I couldn't ruin it for him. So I kept quiet and let him do most of the talking.

He had a lot to say too.

Things like how he wanted me to move in with him.

And he wanted to buy me a car.

There was more…

"You said you were in school in Arizona, right? Business classes, yeah?"

"Um, yeah," I replied.

"Great. Then you can enroll in college here."

I laughed. "Noel, I only have six measly credits. I kind of overstated how far along I was. I've only ever taken two business classes. And those were at my local community college."

"Not a problem. Those credits will transfer."

He was right, they would. I guess it just felt weird having someone believe in me more than I believed in myself.

Maybe this was what I'd needed all along?

I really did want to finish school someday. I was determined to make something of myself, especially since I was finally out of Two Palms. Even if Noel and I worked out, I wanted to always have the ability to stand on my own two feet.

So, yes, school was good.

I was onboard with that.

"Maybe I can apply for a student loan," I mused.

Sitting up next to me, Noel said, "Maisie, you don't have to go into debt. I'll pay for your classes."

It amazed me how he could offer things of that magnitude like it was the most natural thing in the world.

But I shook my head. "No. I can't let you do that."

Perplexed, he asked, "Why not? I have the money."

"I know, but it doesn't feel right. Let me just apply for a loan, okay?"

He acquiesced, but there was one thing on which he held firm.

"You have to move in with me. I won't have you living in this part of town. It's just too dangerous. If something were to happen to you, I'd never forgive myself."

I hesitated, and he laid us back down on our sides so we could face each other.

Quietly, he said, "Maisie, why are you so reluctant to accept my help?"

I looked down, absently picking at a thread on the sheet.

"I don't know. I guess I just don't want to use you. I still feel bad for misleading you in Sweden."

He cupped my face, urging me, "Look at me."

Once our eyes met, he said, "I told you what happened in Sweden does not bother me. I love you, Maisie, and I mean it. You're not using me, okay? This is what people who love each other do for one another. They share what they have and do nice things. So please, let me do this *for* you."

Choking up, I said, "And just what am I supposed to do for you in return? I have nothing to offer."

"Ah, babe"—he wrapped me in a big hug—"and that is where you are wrong. You love me, right?"

I nodded. "I do."

"Then just love me, okay? That's all I ask for in return."

"But I already do," I whispered. "More than you could ever know."

"Good," he said. "Just never stop, then. Never stop and we'll be fine."

32

A LITTLE BIT OF PROGRESS

NOEL

Maisie told me she could keep on loving me.

I promised her in return that I'd never leave her, and I'd be patient with her.

It was true. I would have done anything for her.

We made love again to solidify the promises we'd made, and also because we couldn't keep our hands off of each other.

When morning arrived, Maisie gathered her meager amount of things, and we checked her out for good at the little office in the front of the nondescript motel building.

I knew, despite our promises, it would be an uphill battle for her to feel comfortable with me taking care of things. She was dealing with guilt for having misled me in Stockholm, and had a fiercely independent streak.

There were other things on my mind that morning. I had more to take care of. Like help Maisie go back to school.

On the way to my house, I made a mental note to talk to my sister. I was pretty sure Noelle could help Maisie get into UNLV. She knew just about everyone in the business department, and since classes didn't start for a couple weeks there was a good chance she'd be able to pull a few strings.

Maisie could maybe start this fall.

I decided not to say anything to Maisie just yet. Not only had I not talked to Noelle, but I didn't want to get her hopes up, in case it was a no-go.

As we neared my house, I noticed Maisie was really quiet. When we'd first hopped into the car, she'd grabbed up that stuffed dog she called Claude and proceeded to tell me a little about her childhood.

Suffice it to say, those days weren't the best.

But I wasn't sure what was going on now. Maisie was clutching Claude like her life depended on it, and she was staring out the passenger window, her lips tightly drawn.

"Maisie, don't let your childhood get you down." I reached over and laid what I hoped was a comforting hand on her leggings-clad knee. "The past is the past. And that goes for us too. Whether it's Sweden, or your life as a kid, everything will be fine from here on out. I swear to you."

She smiled over at me, but I knew she was unconvinced.

I kept telling myself it was going to take some time.

Sighing, Maisie said, "Can we just change the subject?"

I nodded. "Sure."

"I don't know if I mentioned it last night," she began, switching gears. "But I have a shift tomorrow at the convenience store."

"All right…"

I wasn't sure where this was going.

"Well," Maisie went on, "the problem is I don't know how I'm going to get there."

"Huh?"

She glanced around the upscale area we'd entered—my neighborhood—and murmured, "It doesn't look like there's a bustling bus service around here."

She was right.

Good thing I had a great alternative in mind.

Trying to contain my enthusiasm, I said, "What's your dream car, Mais?"

She thought it over. "Hmm, I have to say this one's pretty damn nice. I've always loved Porsches."

"Then it's settled." I tapped the steering wheel. "We'll get you one of these. Problem solved."

Her eyes widened as she gaped over at me.

"Are you crazy, Noel? Absolutely not. You can't buy me a car, let alone a freaking Porsche!"

Frustrated, I groaned. "Didn't we just go over this? How people in love do things for each other?"

"Yes, I know, but…" Maisie trailed off, distracted and awed by something.

We'd just pulled up to my house, and she whispered, "Holy shit, Noel."

As we sat in the driveway, Maisie gawked at my house. In her defense, it was rather big and stately, constructed of hand-cut stone and with an impressive arched entryway.

I was used to it, but I could see where others might find it impressive.

Clearly, Maisie did.

"You are so much richer than I realized, Noel," she whispered shakily. "It's kind of scary."

"Scary?" I laughed. "That shouldn't frighten you one bit, babe."

"I know. And it doesn't in the way you might be thinking. It's just scary as in overwhelming."

I was reminded again that this was the reason why I'd agreed to take things slowly. It was the only way it would ever work. Even though I was ready to pick up right where we left off in Sweden, she wasn't.

That was okay. I could wait for her to catch up to where I was.

I decided not to press on the car…for now.

Instead, I said, "I can take you to work tomorrow. I'll pick you up too. You're right, there's no bus service out here."

What I really wanted was for Maisie to ditch her job. There was no need for her to work at the convenience store any longer.

But like with the car, I was tabling that battle for another day.

Maybe once Maisie got into school, she'd give up the convenience store gig.

I hoped so.

"Are you sure taking me to work won't interfere with your schedule?" she replied.

I shook my head. "No, not at all. Training camp hasn't started yet. I've just been going down to the arena on my own to skate and work out."

"Oh, okay."

Wow, that was it?

I couldn't believe Maisie was giving in so easily.

Maybe we were making progress.

And that meant there was hope.

WHO'S IN CHARGE?

MAISIE

What Noel didn't realize was that I *wanted* to take him up on all his generous offers.

I mean, a new Porsche?

Come on. Of course I wanted that.

Who wouldn't?

But I couldn't just say yes, yes, yes.

I felt like I had to earn those things first.

Noel may have said my love for him was more than enough, and he had that for sure, but I felt like I should offer him more.

So that night, while we were eating dinner in his spacious, meticulously appointed dining room, I brought it up.

"I want to do something for you in return, Noel," I said. "If you're going to let me live here, buy me a car, and stuff like that—"

"Wait, are you saying I can buy you the Porsche?" he interrupted, his eyes lighting up.

He was seated across the table from me, looking handsome as hell.

I shrugged and uttered a noncommittal, "Maybe..."

That's all Noel needed to hear.

"Awesome!" he exclaimed. "What color would you want?"

"Uh-uh-uh, not so fast. First, we have to think of some way for me to pay you back."

He smiled over at me mischievously, his gaze dropping to the visible cleavage in my low-cut tank.

"I can think of a few ways right now, Maisie."

"Noel!" I threw a dinner roll at him, which he handily caught. "Sex isn't a good trade-off. Not when I want it from you just as much as you want it from me."

He looked pleasantly surprised. "You do?"

I nodded, and he waggled his brows. "Cool. Then we should just become each other's sex slaves."

"Noel, be serious."

"Okay, okay." He rubbed his lightly stubbled chin. "Let me think..."

I waited patiently, until at last he said, "Tell you what. I *could* use an assistant. Someone to remind me of appointments and appearances, and keep me up-to-date on what the team wants from me and when. That sort of thing."

I liked that idea, and said, "I can definitely do that."

"Good. Then it's settled?"

"Yep." I nodded proudly. "Say hello to your new assistant."

"My new, very hot assistant," he corrected, smiling as he pushed his chair back and stood up.

When he started over to me, I played dumb. "Noel, what ever are you doing?"

"I'm coming over to give my new assistant a kiss, of course."

I teased, "Ah, so you're going to be *that* kind of boss."

When he reached me, he caressed my cheek. "I'll be whatever kind of boss you want me to be, Maisie."

I leaned into him, liking this game. "I'm cool with this version for now," I admitted.

"You are, are you?"

I peered up at him. "Mmm-hmm. These are special circumstances. So, yes, I am."

"In that case, I should definitely kiss you."

"You should," I agreed.

Noel leaned down, touching his lips to mine.

Hell with that!

Plunging my fingers into his hair, I deepened the kiss.

But then I had to break away. Not for any bad reason. It was just that I had come up with an even better idea, one I knew Noel would love.

"Whatcha doing?" he asked.

I raised a brow. "This…"

Sliding down from the chair, I dropped to my knees, putting me perfectly in line with the hardening outline in his dark pants.

Before he could protest—not that I expected him to—I unzipped him and had his cock in my mouth in seconds.

"Jesus, Maisie," he gasped. "You *are* full of surprises."

From that point on, Noel was putty in my hands.

He may have become my boss, but I was the one in charge that night.

YEP, MAISIE IS IN CHARGE

NOEL

Maisie was so funny. She insisted that she work as my assistant for at least a week before we even looked at cars.

Since I didn't have much of a structured schedule yet, there wasn't much for her to do as my assistant.

Still, she wanted to put together a spreadsheet containing all my current workouts and skating sessions. Then she wanted to know what I hoped to achieve with each.

"Shit, you're worse than Coach Townsend," I groused when she made me sit down in my own study, her behind the big oak desk and me across from her like an unruly pupil.

It was only her fifth day on the job, and she had taken to it like a duck to water.

"Just list your goals and objectives for the upcoming season," she said as she tapped away on the laptop I'd given her for her new position. "I'll input those so we can check your progress at regular intervals."

"You're really taking this assistant job seriously," I murmured.

"Of course I am," she retorted.

Stopping what she was doing and peering over at me from across the desk, she said, "That's why I quit the convenience store, remember?"

Ah, the one good thing that had come from Maisie becoming my assistant—she'd quit the Quik-Stop.

The least I could do was humor her and come up with some goals, right?

Scrubbing my hand down my face, I said, "Okay, let me think for a minute."

She leaned back, crossing her arms. "Take your time."

"Well, first and foremost," I began, "I want to win another Stanley Cup. That is definitely goal number one this season."

She rolled her eyes at me. "Noel, that's a goal for you and every other guy on the team. How about giving me something more specific to just you?"

"Okay, okay." I shook my head, chuckling. "Man, you're tough."

Smiling proudly, she said, "Why thank you, Noel. I wasn't kidding when I said I take this job seriously."

"I see that."

It was time to get to work and come up with a few goals, so I thought some more and finally came up with a couple.

"I have some. Are you ready?" I asked.

"I am."

"As an individual, I'd like to become an overall better player. I'd also like to work on becoming a better defense partner to Dylan Culderway."

Nodding, she typed those into the spreadsheet. "Got it."

"Cool."

"I have to say, though, Noel," Maisie went on. "I've been reading up on you and it seems you're already damn good at both those things."

I shrugged. "Yeah, maybe. But there's always room for improvement, right?"

She smiled. "True."

Maisie had no idea I was secretly preening inside.

She'd been reading up on me, eh?

I didn't suck, so most articles tended to be complimentary.

Still, what I'd said was true—I could always be better.

With that in mind, I added, "I should also focus more on my leg strength with my workouts. My whole lower body, really. I'm fast, but I can always be faster. And being stronger gets you there."

Maisie was typing away, nodding satisfactorily as she listened to me list off several more hockey-related goals.

When I finished, she said, "These are all excellent. I'm really proud of you."

"Thanks, Mais."

"Okay, so I'll print out a month-by-month schedule. That is, once I work out the details of how best to keep track of things."

I couldn't deny I was impressed with her level of commitment.

"You're good at this, babe. You should definitely go back for that business degree."

"Thanks." She suddenly looked sad. "I'd like to, but I think it's too late to apply anywhere."

"Uh, maybe not," I stated quietly.

I was tentative, as I wasn't sure how Maisie would react to me offering assistance once again.

"What do you mean?" she asked, brows furrowing.

"Well…" I leaned back and blew out a breath. "…I had a chance to talk with my sister last night. Remember how I told you she's working on her MBA at UNLV?"

"Yes, I remember you saying that."

"I asked her if she could pull some strings and have you put in an expedited application."

I expected Maisie to be wary, but she was surprisingly enthusiastic.

Maybe she really was warming to the idea of accepting my help.

"Oh my God, Noel!" she exclaimed. "That'd be beyond awesome. I'd appreciate it so much. What did Noelle say?"

"She told me she thinks she can help. Just fill out the application online, have your transcript sent from your previous school, then let her know when everything's complete. I'll give you her email."

"Okay." Maisie nodded excitedly. "That sounds easy enough."

"Once that's done, Noelle can talk with the people who move these things along."

Biting her lip, Maisie said, "I'd probably only want to take a couple of classes the first semester, just to ease my way back in. I think too that it's too late to apply for financial aid. But maybe I can get a small personal loan. Can you vouch as my employer?"

"Of course," I replied.

I decided not to fight her on the loan thing. I'd probably have to co-sign for her to actually get any kind of bank to give her money, anyway.

We'd just cross that bridge when we came to it.

"However you'd like to do it is fine with me," I said.

Maisie liked the cautious approach, and that was fine. I was just happy she was feeling more at ease with me helping.

That led me to ask, "How about if we move up car shopping day? If you take classes at the university, you're going to need a way to get there and back."

Considering, she said, "Hmm, you do have a point."

"So what do you say, Mais?"

She blew out a breath, looked over at me, and replied, "Okay. Let's do it."

Yes!

35

GETTING READY

MAISIE

Noel bought me a Porsche, a Panamera like his, but in blue instead of red.

Before everything was decided, I'd gone round and round about the color. I liked the blue shades, of which there were two, but I couldn't decide whether to go with the light or dark hue.

Noel settled it for me.

Amused, he'd said at the dealership, "Babe, you kind of have to choose the dark blue."

"Why's that?" I'd asked, perplexed.

With the sweetest smile, he replied, "Because it matches your eyes."

I was surprised he'd even noticed such a thing.

"Really, it does?"

"Uh-huh."

The look of love and excitement he'd had on his handsome face, as we stood there in the showroom, made the decision easy.

"Dark blue it is, then," I declared.

That Panamera was what I was driving in now. It was a couple of weeks later, and I was on my way to my first class at UNLV.

Yep, I'd been accepted to their business school.

Yay!

Noel's sister had totally come through.

As for the tuition cost, I had scrapped the idea of securing a loan and instead worked out a reduction in my pay from Noel, in order to defray what he ended up fronting for me.

Someday, I planned to pay him back in full.

Maybe that sounded silly, but it made me feel better.

The semester was starting before Labor Day. I'd stuck with my original plan to not take too many classes. So I had three that met three days a week, leaving me plenty of time to continue as Noel's assistant.

Speaking of which…

As I'd immersed myself more in that role, I'd discovered Noel was pretty business savvy. The guy was loaded far beyond his impressive hockey salary, having invested wisely in real estate.

He had a beach property located on a private island in Florida. One of his hockey friends, Jaxon Holland, had spent the summer down there. He'd also met a girl. But I didn't know too much about that.

So, recognizing that Noel was no slouch when it came to finances, I decided I should be the best assistant possible for him.

He deserved nothing less.

As a result, my days were filled with organizing and arranging many things. Hockey preseason and training camp were quickly approaching, and that meant I was busier than ever.

There were tons of upcoming promotional work-related things for the players, like photo shoots, filming promo clips to run on TV, recording radio spots, interviews, and so on. Workouts on and off the ice had picked up in frequency and intensity too.

Noel was as busy as I was.

It was the main reason why we were pumped for the one day we both had off—Labor Day. There were plans in place to attend a big barbeque picnic that the Wolves captain, Brent Oliver, and his wife, Aubrey, were hosting at their house.

It would be my first opportunity to meet Noel's teammates.

Besides my one chance encounter with Blake Cavaletti, I'd met no one else.

To say I was nervous would've been an understatement.

I thought about it all day on my first day of school, and also the entire week and weekend leading up. As the barbeque grew near, I became more and more nervous.

Noel insisted it'd all be fine.

I sure hoped so.

And then it finally arrived—Labor Day.

On the morning of the barbeque, I stepped into the big walk-in closet in the bedroom I shared with Noel and flipped through my meager assortment of clothes.

After a minute, I groaned, "What in the hell am I supposed to wear to this thing? I have absolutely nothing good."

Noel, typical guy, was already dressed and ready. Men had it so easy. A pair of khaki cargo shorts, a white polo shirt, and some beat-up Chucks, and he was ready to roll.

Me, I still had a long way to go. My hair needed to be brushed out, I had makeup to put on, and, of course, I still needed to choose a damn outfit.

Stepping into the closet, Noel came up from behind me and wrapped his arms around me.

I leaned back into him.

"Seriously," I huffed. "I want to make a good impression at this barbeque."

"Mmm…" He nuzzled my neck. "Maybe you should just wear what you have on."

"Yeah, right," I scoffed.

Noel was silly. What I had on was a short robe and nothing else. I'd stepped out of the shower only moments earlier.

I had to laugh, though.

I wouldn't have on even that much if he kept up what he was doing—slipping his hand under the yellow terrycloth and caressing my breasts.

As much as I wanted to continue, I had to make him stop. If he didn't, we'd never make it to the barbeque.

"Noel, don't," I moaned halfheartedly, moving his hand away and readjusting the tie on the robe. "There's no time for this. I have to get ready."

I spun around to face him and he raised a brow, challenging me.

"Funny. You don't *sound* like you want to stop."

"I don't," I admitted. "But we have to."

Sighing, he gave in. "You're right."

He backed away from me, like he had to or his resistance would crumble.

I knew the feeling.

With a hungry gaze he couldn't extinguish, he assured me, "Just so you know, this isn't over. I am totally devouring that hot little bod of yours tonight."

I laughed. "I have no objections to that."

"Somehow I didn't think you would."

He was giving me that look again, the one that always left me aching for him.

I was tempted to suggest scrapping the barbeque and spending the whole day in bed. But I really wanted to meet his friends and teammates.

Reluctantly, I pushed him farther away. "You are so bad. Quit staring at me like that."

"Wait, what'd I do?"

Noel loved to play innocent, and I loved calling him out on it.

"Ha, like you don't know. Stop tempting me with your sex-eyes and help me pick out an outfit."

He chuckled. "All right, sweetheart. Let's see what you got."

He stepped forward again, and we browsed through my clothes, eventually finding something I liked—a fun, frilly sundress in pastel watercolors.

Noel liked it too.

"That's perfect," he said.

As I slipped it on, smoothing the light cotton material down into place, he joined me, running his hand down my side. "You look so beautiful, Maisie."

I laughed. "But I haven't even put any makeup on yet. And my hair's still an unruly mess."

"An unruly hot mess," he corrected.

"Oh, stop."

He turned serious. "Maisie, you don't need any of those things. You're stunning as you are."

"Thanks," I murmured.

Wow, this man truly loved me.

Nonetheless, even though Noel didn't think I needed those things, I still lined my eyes, applied a few coats of mascara, and glossed my lips. And then I brushed out and styled my hair.

Good thing the gloss I used was the kind that didn't come off easily, as Noel insisted on kissing me like crazy before we left the house.

"You're out of control." I teased, pushing him away so we could walk to the car.

"Out of control in love," he volleyed back, leaning in for one more kiss.

"Noel," I warned.

"Okay, sweetheart…" He took my hand in his. "…come on. Let's go introduce my gorgeous girl to the team."

BRENT'S BARBEQUE

NOEL

Not all of my teammates were at the barbeque, but quite a few were there. I introduced Maisie to Dylan Culderway, Benny Perry, Nolan Solvenson, Brent Oliver, Blake Cavaletti, and so many more. All of those guys' significant others were at Brent's too.

Maisie was tentative with everyone at first. But as time wore on, she began mingling on her own, hitting it off with everyone.

She sure was coming out of her shell and taking to this, her new life.

I loved it.

Whenever I was caught up in conversation, Maisie would peel away and easily find someone to chat with.

But the one person she hung out with the most, by far, was Noelle.

I was glad my twin was at the barbeque. But I sure hadn't expected her to be. I had no clue how she had come to be invited. It wasn't like she was dating any of the players or anything.

Or was she?

I had to find out.

So I went to look for her.

Of course, I found her with Maisie, standing over by the swimming pool, chatting and giggling over something.

I reached them and uttered a quick, "Hey, what's up?"

Then I flat-out asked Noelle who had invited her.

Looking away, she replied sheepishly, "Uh, Blake did."

I was stunned. "What? Cavaletti invited you?"

"Uh-huh."

She was being uncharacteristically evasive, so I glanced across the lawn at Blake—tall, dark, handsome bastard that he was.

He better not be banging my sister!

I had no chance to ask how Noelle knew him, because she and Maisie suddenly just *had* to go to the ladies' room.

Yeah, right.

Their girl code had been activated.

But I was onto their ploy.

Before they made their getaway, I stepped in front of them, stopping their progress.

"Whoa, wait up a sec," I said. "I have a question."

"What is it, Noel?" my sister asked, aggravated.

"Just what is it with you ladies always running off to the bathroom together? Are there, like, secret meetings in there or something?"

Maisie interjected, "Nice try, Noel."

Totally onto me, she grabbed Noelle's hand.

As they brushed past me, my sister cooed, "We'll never tell."

Those two, I had to laugh. It had been a good evasive move on their part, working spectacularly.

My sister and Maisie ought to be on the damn hockey team. They sure think like defensive players.

Chuckling as I imagined the two of them back-checking opponents, I went to seek out the guys. I was now in the mood to talk hockey, which worked out well since I came upon Dylan and Brent and could hear them discussing the upcoming season.

"I think we're much stronger with the trade we made this summer." I overheard Brent say to Dylan.

"Absolutely," he agreed. "Blake Cavaletti is a great addition."

When I walked up to them, my teammates gave me nods of acknowledgment.

Brent then asked, "Are you enjoying the barbeque so far, Sandlund?"

"You bet your ass I am," I replied.

"Good."

Waving my arm at the expansive desert gardens that comprised Brent's large backyard, I added, "It's been great seeing everyone here today."

"It has," Brent agreed. "And by the way, Maisie is amazing."

I let out a contented sigh. "Yeah, she really is. I'm glad she's fitting in."

The talk then turned back to hockey.

"So you think we got it in us for another Stanley Cup run?" Brent asked.

"I do." I nodded. "I really do."

Dylan agreed, "Yeah, I see no reason why we can't go all the way this year."

After a moment of thought, Brent asked me, "Hey, you played with the new guy in Sweden, right?"

"Yes," I confirmed.

"How'd he look over there on the ice?"

"Fantastic," I answered truthfully. "Blake Cavaletti was one of our best players."

Brent was pleased. "Cool. I'm glad to hear that."

I reiterated how Blake was an absolute stellar addition to the team, adding, "He's a much better player than Drew Chidders."

"He seems to have a better attitude too," Dylan said, chuckling. "I get the impression he's a good dude."

"He is," I said.

As long as he stays away from my sister, I thought to myself.

I glanced around, looking for Noelle and Maisie. I hadn't seen either of them since they'd come back from the bathroom.

But had they even ever returned?

I didn't think so.

Okay, this was strange.

What could possibly have been keeping them?

37

BAD TIMING

MAISIE

I was having the best time at the barbeque. Everyone was so much nicer than I'd expected them to be. I'd obviously psyched myself out with my silly, unfounded concerns.

It was all good. I fit right in with the Wolves' players and their significant others.

Maybe Noel and I really would work out in the long run?

And maybe, just maybe, I truly deserved him.

I hoped so, as not only had I fallen more in love with him, I freaking adored his sister.

Noelle and I had just really clicked.

At first I'd been intimidated.

She was so damn beautiful, tall like Noel, statuesque even. And she had the most gorgeous platinum-blonde hair, as well as the same striking blue eyes Noel had.

Noelle also had a figure to die for.

I quickly discovered, though, that she, much like her brother, was as beautiful on the inside as the outside. Noelle was down-to-earth and easy to talk to. I had a feeling we would end up becoming great friends.

As it was, we already had our girl code down pat.

When Noel put his twin on the spot about Blake, a guy I could tell she was into, I used the tried and true we-have-to-go-to-the-bathroom excuse. Always a good one.

Noelle caught on right away and murmured a sly, "Thank you."

Noel didn't even notice, as he was trying to delay us by asking something about why girls always go to the bathroom together.

We got away, and now we were on our way to the bathroom behind the pool house, the closest one.

Noelle and I congratulated ourselves on our successful escape.

"That move worked out well, Maisie. I really do have to pee," Noelle said as we reached the tiny bathroom in the back of the pool house. "So what you told Noel *was* technically true."

"I'm glad it wasn't a lie," I stated honestly.

I was trying to be nothing but honest with Noel these days, so it was good to know I hadn't misled him.

Since the bathroom looked like it could comfortably fit only one person at a time, I hung back and said to Noelle, "I'll wait out here for you, okay?"

"Okay, cool," she replied.

Once she was inside the bathroom, my phone started ringing.

Huh, who could that be?

I thought it might be a wrong number since all the important people in my life were at the barbeque.

But then I saw the number.

My heart sank.

It was my mom.

"What the hell does she want?" I hissed under my breath, stepping farther away.

I knew this couldn't be anything good. I hadn't heard one word from her since I'd been back. She didn't care where my life led me.

That wasn't surprising, but it still hurt.

But here she was now, calling me out of the blue. Probably only to drive the stake a little farther into my heart.

Maybe I shouldn't answer.

A part of me felt obligated to, though. Terrible or not, she was still my mother.

So, sighing resignedly, I took her call, deciding, however, to act nonchalant. Like we'd talked days ago, not months.

Why give her the satisfaction of anything else?

"Hey, Mom, what's up?" I said breezily.

My mother, in usual fashion, played right along with our friendly farce.

"Maisie, I'm so glad you answered. It's wonderful hearing your voice."

Yeah, right.

"You too, Mom." I coughed.

There was an uncomfortable silence, until she said, "So where are you these days?"

"I'm in Las Vegas."

"Ah, interesting. I guess that guy who came out to the trailer found you, huh?"

"He did."

"That's nice." She sighed. "Do you live with him now?"

"I do. Not that it's any of your business."

"Maisie," she chastised.

Oh, hell, I was tiring of these fake niceties. I knew she hadn't called to catch up.

So I flat-out asked, "Why are you calling, Mom?"

"Well, I have some news."

"What kind of news?"

"I wanted to let you know Gary and I are back together."

Ah, so she managed to lure the ole Juice King back in.

"That's wonderful, Mom," I stated sarcastically.

Ignoring my cynicism, she exclaimed, "I know, right? It's so great."

Weary, I replied, "Why are you calling *me* with this news?"

She sniffed. "You are my daughter, Maisie."

I'd had enough.

"That's funny," I snapped. "You made it pretty clear to my boyfriend—you know, that guy who came to see you—that you were cutting all ties with me."

"Oh, that." She snickered. "I was just mad at you at the time. And how could you blame me? You didn't come back to help with the bills or anything. Not even when I continued to pay for your cell phone."

I wished she could see me roll my eyes.

"Mom, you only paid for that because you had a good deal with the carrier."

"So? I was still paying."

I sighed.

She was impossible.

"It doesn't matter," I said. "I pay for it now."

I'd made that change after I'd moved in with Noel.

"Okay, okay, you're right. It's not important. But I could certainly be mad at you for something else."

"Oh, what's that?" I asked dryly.

"You screwed things up for me and Gary in Sweden, for one. I'm still angry about that, young lady."

Unbelievable!

"*I* screwed things up?" I hissed quietly, so as not to draw attention.

I was alone since this was the back of the pool house and surrounded by palm trees. Still, I kept my voice hushed. The conversation was becoming too heated.

I also stepped over to a clump of cacti, and then said to my impossible mother, "How is Gary dumping you *my* fault? His stupid accountant told me you and he had broken up weeks before I was kicked out of that suite."

"Yes," Mom conceded, "that's true. But the fact I'd kept you a secret in the first place angered Gary so much that it caused our first really *huge* fight. That was more our undoing than why we'd broken up in the first place."

I shook my head, amazed, but not in a good way.

I was holding up well as far as my mother could tell, but inside I was on the verge of tears. This wasn't good. Noelle would be out of the bathroom any second.

I needed to pull it together.

Also, what if someone came back here?

There was no need to ruin everyone's good time with my ridiculous family drama.

To wrap things up, since they'd gone downhill, I said quietly into the phone, "Mom, we'll have to talk later. This is not a good time to discuss this crap."

"Fine, Maisie. It's not why I'm calling, anyway."

Ah, we were finally getting to the truth.

"So why *are* you calling?" I asked warily.

"I'm calling to let you know I found more of your clothes. I've been cleaning up the trailer since I plan to sell it soon, and I came across a few things I must've missed the first go-round. Anyway, there are a few photo albums I also thought you might like to have." Softly, she added, "Your dad's in them."

Oh, hell.

There was the final push of the stake into my heart. I really wanted those albums.

My mother knew all along I'd cave hearing about those. That was why she'd saved it for last.

The clothes I couldn't care less about, but something more to connect me with the guy who had fathered me?

Yes, that was something I desperately wanted.

She had me, and she knew it.

Surrendering, I agreed to come out to the trailer.

"You're going to have to make it quick," Mom informed me. "I'm leaving to meet up with Gary sometime tomorrow."

I really did have to move fast. Mom would leave on a dime. And she'd toss my stuff out so fast it wouldn't be funny. That would include the photo albums.

"Okay," I said, "I can leave right now. I'll see you later today, Mom."

"Great, Maisie. See you soon. Bye."

Just as I was disconnecting and lowering the phone, Noelle found me.

"Hey, what are you doing hiding all the way over here?" she asked, perplexed.

Then she saw the expression on my face.

"Wait. Are you all right, Maisie? What happened? You look really messed up right now."

"I am messed up," I whispered, holding up the phone. "I was just talking to my mom."

It was evident from her sigh that Noel had filled her in on my lovely mother.

"I should ask first if she's okay," Noelle began.

I nodded. "Uh-huh. She's fine. She just got back with her boyfriend. And she called to tell me she's leaving tomorrow, for good."

"Wow. No way."

"Yeah," I sighed. "She wants me to go out to Two Palms to pick up some of my things."

I closed my eyes, and, as the gravity of the situation hit me, I lamented, "I guess this really is goodbye for her and me."

I thought I was done with my mother, but a part of me had always believed I could reconnect with her if I wanted to.

This felt so final.

It hurt that I seemed to care for her far more than she cared for me.

Once that sunk in, I let out a choked sob.

Noelle put her arm around me. "Aw, honey, it'll be okay. Still, I think we should go find Noel."

"Yeah, I think so too."

38

SHOULD I GO?

NOEL

Just as I was about to go search for my sister and Maisie, they returned from their bathroom run. Even from across the lawn, though, it was clear something was terribly wrong.

I started over to them, noticing Noelle giving me a take-it-easy-Noel look.

Quickly turning my rapid pace to a casual stroll, I smiled like everything was okay. There was no reason to upset Maisie any further. And upset she was. That was obvious from the strained look on her face.

I was glad the other partygoers were too preoccupied with having fun to pay her any heed.

"Hey, babe," I stated calmly once I reached Maisie and my sister.

"Hi, Noel," Maisie replied flatly.

Shit, something was definitely awry.

Placing a comforting hand on Maisie's arm, I asked, "Is everything all right, sweetheart?"

She shook her head as she handed me her phone.

When I glanced down at it, I saw right away what had upset her—the last incoming call was from her mother.

Hell.

I'd met the woman only once, and to say she was abrasive would have been a huge understatement.

"Jesus." I frowned down at the screen. "What did *she* want?"

Maisie murmured, "She wants me to go out there."

"What, to Two Palms?"

"Uh-huh."

I remembered all too well how Maisie's mother had so callously handed over her daughter's clothes, and Claude, and I immediately bristled.

"What the fuck for?" I bit out.

"Noel," my sister warned.

Maisie waved her hand. "No, no, it's okay. Noel's right to be aggravated. Lord knows I am. And as to what my mother wanted, she hooked back up with the Juice King and just couldn't wait to share the news."

"Ugh."

I could see where this was going.

"Anyway," Maisie went on, "she called to inform me she's leaving for good. I think it's for real because she's selling the trailer. She has more clothes for me, plus some other stuff—a few photo albums that my dad's in."

Ah, I knew Maisie wanted those.

Noelle and I exchanged looks, and she nodded knowingly.

She excused herself then so Maisie and I could talk just the two of us.

One thing about being a twin was that there really was an unspoken connection. Noelle had known exactly how long to stick around. Once Maisie's absent father had been brought up, with one shared look, she recognized it was a subject best discussed alone between me and Maisie.

She was right.

Maisie's father may have been gone from her life, but he was still important to her. Hell, she freaking loved that tattered and torn stuffed dog he'd given her all those years ago. Claude sat out on our bed every day.

So, as we stood facing each other, I knew I couldn't say *don't go to Two Palms*.

But I sure as fuck wanted to.

Maisie was making such amazing progress in moving past her misplaced guilt. Better yet, she no longer felt it mattered that we'd come from different worlds. We were meant to be together, and she knew it.

But all that was now in jeopardy. Her ridiculous mom could easily set her back.

Still, I knew this was something Maisie had to face. She needed a clean slate to move forward and be 100 percent in our relationship.

And if that meant making peace with her mom, so be it.

Resigned this was the only way, I said, "So when are you planning to go out to Two Palms?"

Maisie's eyes met mine, apology in her indigo depths. "I need to go today. My mom's leaving tomorrow."

I kind of lost it then.

"That damn woman! Talk about waiting till the last minute to hit you with the news."

Maisie laughed bitterly. "I know, right?"

Quietly, I asked, "Do you want me to go with you?"

She shook her head. "No, I don't think so. I need to do this on my own."

"Are you sure? 'Cause I can leave this party right now, no problem."

"No, Noel. Stay with your sister and your friends."

Since I'd driven, I fished the Porsche key fob from my jeans pocket.

Handing it over to Maisie, along with her phone, I said, "Here, take my car. It'll be quicker than me driving you home to get yours."

She hesitated. "Are you sure? How will you get back to the house?"

Aw, she was so cute., still worrying about me even when she had so much on her plate.

Chuckling, I assured her, "I'll have Noelle drive me back. Don't worry about me."

"Oh, okay. I didn't think about that."

I could see Maisie was distracted. As not only did I have Noelle, any one of the guys would drive me home.

I didn't mention that. It wasn't important.

I did ask Maisie to keep me updated, and for her to call if she needed anything.

"I mean it, Mais. Anything at all."

"Okay, Noel. I will."

I kissed her, and she turned to leave.

"Talk to you soon," she murmured.

"Okay."

As I watched her walk away, I hoped and prayed this woman I loved like nobody's business would finally find the closure she needed for herself…and for us.

39

CLOSURE? MAYBE NOT

MAISIE

I was on my way to Two Palms, the wide desert expanse before me as I barreled down the highway at eighty in Noel's Porsche.

Maybe if I went fast enough, I could outrun myself.

That's when it hit me—that's what this had always been about. My back and forth with Noel, my constant wavering, it was me running from myself.

Ugh, but I couldn't think about that now.

I had to deal with my mom first.

As I crossed the state line into Arizona, I thought about how I hadn't expected to return so soon, and certainly not under these circumstances.

I always believed that if and when I came back, it'd be on my own terms.

Ah, but life never works like that, does it?

No, especially not when dealing with my mother.

"Our dynamic is so messed up," I murmured out loud.

The whole thing was ridiculous—Mom running away with the Juice King. I had to laugh.

My amusement didn't last long. It faded the instant I reached Two Palms.

"Yay," I muttered sarcastically as I drove through the run-down town. "I'm back."

I passed the convenience store where I once worked and the gas station where my first boyfriend once pumped gas.

One time he had pumped me in the back room…after hours, of course.

That was a story I planned to keep to myself. I didn't think Noel would want to hear that one.

By the time I pulled up to the trailer I once called home, I felt ill and out of sorts. Maybe coming back had been a big mistake.

All it was doing so far was reminding me of just how different Noel and I were.

I thought I was past that.

Maybe it wasn't that easy to escape your demons. You probably have to have truly dealt with them to move on.

And I had not.

That's when it happened—everything I'd worked so hard to overcome came rushing back over me, not unlike a huge wave in the ocean, knocking me down, pulling me under.

I knew then that all the fears I thought I'd squashed had just been kept at bay. And now they were back with a vengeance.

Once I was out of the car and knocking on the front door of the trailer, all of which felt like a hazy dream, I was emotionally right back to the day Noel had found me.

"This isn't good."

No, it wasn't.

No one was coming to the door, so I knocked again, frantically this time. All the while, my heart was screaming for me to turn around and leave. Two Palms had me spiraling, and I feared what my mother might say to really bring me down. She had the ability to make my whole relationship implode.

I should have left, but I didn't.

It was too late, anyway. Mom had opened the door.

"Maisie," she said.

I gave her a curt nod. "Mom."

After an assessing once-over, she clucked, "Huh. For someone who just nabbed herself a hot and famous hockey player, you sure look miserable."

I rolled my eyes.

This was so typical.

"Hello to you too, Mom," I scoffed.

Waving her hand, her blood-red nails a quick blur, she stated dismissively, "Good God, Maisie, you are entirely too serious. I'm only having a little fun with you. Why are you knocking anyway?" She moved aside. "Get in here."

I stepped into the trailer and it felt like déjà vu.

No, not that, since I had, in fact, lived there.

It was just weird, that was all.

I glanced around.

Nothing had changed. Same old faded floral print sofa, same old worn red vinyl chair wedged in the corner. The kitchen was on the right, and to the left, a skinny hall bisected the living room, leading to two small bedrooms and one cramped bath.

Mom picked up a pack of smokes from a nearby table. She lit one and plopped down on the sofa. She was wearing tight blue jeans and a bronze sweater. She looked good, as always, like an older version of me.

Eyeing me intently, she said, "From that look on your face, I guess you're used to mansions and luxury now." She flicked an ash on the carpeted, albeit threadbare, floor. "I have to say, you did good, Maisie. I'm proud of you."

I rolled my eyes.

Leave it to Mom to think I was with Noel for his money.

But there was something else I thought of then.

"Wait. How do you know so much about Noel?"

She took a drag from her smoke, flicked an ash, this time into a tray on the little end table next to her, and said, "I met the guy, remember?"

"Yes, I know. But he told me he didn't mention that he plays hockey."

Mom rolled her eyes. They were the same indigo color I saw reflected back at me every day when I looked in the mirror. It was amazing how we could look so much alike, yet be so different.

She blew out a breath. "Right, that's true. He didn't tell me he was a hockey player. But he did mention his name. I, of course, looked him up on Google the minute he left."

Ah, it was all making sense now.

She shrugged, chuckling. "Noel Sandlund, huh? I figured he had to be somebody special to be driving a top-line Porsche like the one he had that day. Speaking of which, I noticed you drove here in the same car. That guy must really trust you, letting you tool around in a car like that."

"He does trust me," I snapped.

"Anyway," Mom went on, "I thought he might be some kind of a Las Vegas businessman or something. Imagine my surprise when I discovered he's far more than that—he's one of the Las Vegas Wolves' premiere defensemen."

"That's not why I'm with him, Mother," I clarified.

I was tired of her alluding to as much. Landing wealthy men was her gig, not mine.

I added, "I'd be with Noel even if he worked at a gas station."

My mother snipped, "If I recall, you've been there, done that."

Ugh.

I'd had enough.

"Mom, just shut up," I snapped.

I hadn't come to argue. I just wanted to get my clothes and the photo albums, then say goodbye, possibly for good.

"Where are you going with Gary?" I asked, partly to change the subject and partly out of curiosity. "Will you be heading back to Sweden?"

Mom shook her head, took one last hit of her mostly spent cigarette, and put it out in the ashtray.

"No, no," she said. "Gary's permanent residence is in LA. We'll be living there."

"Ah, I see."

"You and Noel can come visit us, if you'd like," she said, surprising the hell out of me.

But she was back to typical Mom form when she added, "I bet Gary's place is bigger than your Noel's."

"It's not a competition, Mom," I reminded her. "And he's not *my* Noel. He's just Noel."

"I beg to differ, Mais. I'd say that boy is smitten. Driving all the way out here to find you, moving you into his house, letting you drive his fancy car. He's definitely into you, making him, in my book, *your* Noel."

Ha, if she knew he'd bought me my own Porsche, she'd really flip out. Still, it wasn't what she thought, and I tried to explain.

"Mom, you just don't get it, do you? Yes, Noel loves me. But I love him too."

She put her hand over her heart. "What? You think I don't love Gary?"

It wasn't worth it; she'd never understand.

I shrugged, and she stood up, huffing indignantly. "Let me go get your stuff, Maisie."

"Fine."

Everything was always a battle with her. I prayed I wouldn't end up like that. I didn't want to ever be so bitter.

But I could see where it could happen. I was already feeling angry and resentful right then.

When I left, five minutes later with my things in hand and a shaky promise to keep in touch, I couldn't help but feel bereft. The visit had not gone as planned. There'd been no closure at all. If anything, the old wounds had opened back up.

And they were now bleeding.

I knew closure was what Noel was hoping for. He wanted me to go to Two Palms and finally bid adieu to my old life.

But it wasn't that easy.

Two Palms was just as much a part of me as Chicago was to him. And no matter how much I hated to admit it, I *was* like my mom.

Had I not started my relationship with Noel under false premises?

Yes, yes I had.

He claimed it didn't matter, but what if it did?

What if, in time, he'd come to resent me?

I loved Noel, but would it ever really be enough?

Was I even good for him?

It seemed he might truly be better off without me.

And that broke my heart.

BACK TO WHERE WE WERE

NOEL

I thought Maisie's trip out to Two Palms would be good for her.

Was I ever wrong!

She returned more distant than ever, throwing the photo albums and clothes into the closet, not wanting to look at them or anything. Worse yet, she wouldn't talk about what had gone down, no matter how hard I tried to broach the subject.

"Mais, are you sure there's not something on your mind that you'd like to share? You haven't said much about your visit to your mom."

It was about our tenth conversation on the subject, and like all the others, she replied, "No, there's nothing to talk about. I told you everything went fine, Noel."

I was more adamant this time, though.

"Yes, you keep saying that. But you seem different since you've been back."

She kissed me and patted my arm. "You're sweet to worry. But I'm good, I swear. I just have a lot on my mind."

"Hmm…"

I bet she did, and I bet it would end up not being good for us.

I was ready to press, but glancing down at her watch, Maisie trilled, "Ooh, would you look at the time. It's almost seven thirty. I better get to class. And you"—she eyed me seriously—"you'll be late for practice if you don't get a move on right now, mister. I am still your assistant, you know."

"Yes." I blew out an I-give-up breath. "I know."

That's how we rolled for the next few weeks, going through the motions of everyday life, but not really communicating about anything of substance.

I knew we couldn't go on like that forever.

Something had to break.

I just prayed it wouldn't be us that shattered into a million pieces.

I tried to give Maisie her space, thinking maybe she'd work through whatever was bothering her on her own.

Good thing I had a lot to keep me busy during that time.

Training camp was finishing up, and the regular season started in a week. We had one final preseason home game against the Coyotes first, though.

And it was tonight.

The Coyotes were one of our biggest rivals. It didn't matter that it was still the preseason. The fans would be pumped.

Boy was I ever right.

Even before the game got underway that evening, as I was skating out onto the ice for warm-ups, the Wolves fan base was already fired the fuck up.

The arena was raucous, it was loud.

But I loved it.

If this was a preview of what the regular season would be like, then greatness was in store.

Yeah, I can live with that.

As I was daydreaming about hoisting another Stanley Cup, Blake skated by, tapping my stick with his.

"Hey," he called out as he skated up ahead of me.

I caught up to him, and I could tell right away from the look on his face that he was as psyched as I was.

Sure enough, he said, "Fuck, Noel. Can you believe this crowd tonight? This is amazing."

I chuckled. "Just wait till the regular season starts, my man. This is nothing."

He laughed, assuring me, "I can't wait."

Neither could I.

Blake, taking in the cheering crowd once more, said, "I guess we better not screw it up this year, huh?"

"For sure," I snorted.

Once the game got underway, the lively atmosphere grew even livelier. Our team looked good and we were giving the fans exactly what they wanted.

It was like everyone was in perfect sync.

The poor Coyotes never stood a chance.

Even at the start of the game, our captain, Brent, got a goal.

That was only one minute in.

And then, *bam*, he scored another six minutes later.

When Blake scored in the second period, I got the assist.

In the third, Brent racked up yet another goal, earning him a hat trick.

Ball caps rained down onto the ice.

And then it was over—we had won.

It was glorious, an ideal way to close out our preseason—with a decisive and fun win.

In the locker room, Coach Townsend was more than pleased and congratulated everyone on the stellar game.

Ever the forward-thinking coach, he drew up some plays on the big dry-erase board attached to the wall.

"I liked what I saw out there, boys," he began. "But there's always room for improvement."

Ugh.

His words reminded me of the time Maisie had called me into the study to discuss my goals and objectives for the season. She'd been so cute that day. And she'd said the same thing. Or maybe I had. I couldn't remember.

It all seemed so far away.

I sighed, and Coach's voice became a distant murmur.

Maisie and I just had to get back to where we were.

I loved her too much for us to keep going on like this.

I knew then what I had to do—I had to make her talk to me, no matter what. Waiting for things to improve on their own just wasn't working.

No more delays.

We're talking tonight!

THIS ENDS TONIGHT

MAISIE

I went to Noel's last preseason game to watch him play amazingly. It wasn't just him that was on fire. The whole team seemed destined for greatness.

What was less clear was *our* future.

We were stuck.

I tried to cast the doubts from my mind, but I couldn't. So I made some decisions, important ones that needed to be discussed as soon as possible.

Seemed, though, I wasn't the only one.

When Noel and I were driving back to the house after the game, he told me *he* wanted to talk.

Perfect.

Nodding in agreement, I replied, "Sounds good. I have some

things I need to say too."

He glanced over at me curiously. "You do? Like what?"

Poor Noel.

He'd been waiting, wanting me to talk for a long time now, ever since I'd returned from my mother's.

I hadn't felt ready, though, up until now. I'd been unsure of what to do, or what to say.

But I finally knew what had to be done.

The car, though, wasn't the place for such an important conversation.

So I said, "I think we should wait till we're back at the house to really get into it, Noel."

A flash of irritation crossed his face. "Whatever, Maisie," he snapped.

He was quiet then.

Who could blame him?

None of this was his fault.

In fact, Noel had been nothing but kind and patient ever since the fateful trip to my mom's house.

And that had been three weeks ago.

Somehow, though, I knew it'd come to this.

And what was "this"?

Well, I was going to tell Noel I decided to move out of his place. Not because I didn't love him anymore, but because I loved him too much.

He deserved so much more than broken me. It was time for us to be done.

At that thought, my eyes filled with tears.

We were just pulling into the garage, and shit, I didn't want Noel to see me like this. So I popped open the door and took off.

I was a runner at heart.

Though I knew Noel would follow.

He always did.

And I was right.

He was on my heels as I made my way into the house and to the staircase leading to the second floor.

When I started up the steps, he did too, grinding out a frustrated, "Jesus, Maisie, what the hell is going on? Would you please stop?"

"No," I cried out as I kept moving. "I can't."

If I did, I'd lose my resolve.

And this needed to be done.

Flying into the bedroom that we shared, I grabbed my suitcase from the closet and tossed it onto the bed.

It popped open, like it always did.

I began immediately throwing clothes into the bag.

Out of the corner of my eye, I could see Noel, standing there, watching, stunned.

He pulled himself together quickly, though.

Tightly, he asked, "Why are you packing? Is it because I said I wanted to talk? Funny, 'cause you told me you had some things to say too."

Still tossing clothes into the suitcase, I replied, "I do have some things to say. It was going to be a lot, but I think it's best to keep it short and sweet—I made a decision."

"What kind of decision?" he asked warily.

I blew out a breath, and said in a rush, "I made the decision to leave. And as you can see, that's what I'm doing."

He stepped over to the bed, his eyes pleading. "Maisie, come on now. This is crazy."

"Is it, though?"

There was a blouse in my hand, and I held onto it tightly, like an anchor.

"It was bound to come to this, Noel," I whispered. "Why not get it over with? We are done."

He took a step back, like I'd just smacked him. "Why would you say that, Maisie?"

That kind of did me in. My initial surge of adrenaline plummeted, and I sunk down to the edge of the bed, the blouse I'd been clinging to so tightly dropping to the floor.

My anchor was gone.

Suddenly exhausted, I said softly, "I'll never be right for you, Noel."

He sat down next to me. "Don't I get to be the judge of that?"

"Yes. You just don't see it yet. Trust me, you will."

Sighing, he reached over and took my hand.

I let him, as I had no energy left to fight.

"You're wrong, sweetheart," he said. "I love you. I know those words get tossed around a lot, but I mean them. I love you. I *love you*. Nothing could *ever* change that."

I wanted to believe him, but I felt so damaged.

"We're too different, Noel," I threw out. "I realized that when I was at my mom's. I mean, I *really* realized it. I'd known it all along, I think. That's why I was always so back-and-forth. I was doing my best to ignore our issues, *my* issues. But that day, they became crystal clear to me."

"Ah." He patted my hand. "I understand now what happened."

"You do?"

Squeezing my hand, he said gently, "Yes. But just because two people grow up in different worlds, it doesn't mean they're not meant to be together."

I looked over at him and shook my head. "You're such a romantic, Noel. Shouldn't that be my role in this relationship?"

He smiled. "It's the twenty-first century, babe. Get with the program. Men can be romantics too."

That made me laugh. "I know. I was just kidding."

My laughter then turned to tears.

As I cried, Noel cooed, "Maisie, Maisie, come here. Let me hold you."

I gave in. I didn't really *want* to leave this man. I just didn't know what to do anymore.

So I did the only thing I could—I poured my heart out to him. In the hopes that maybe, just maybe, there was a chance for me to get past this, for real, and for good.

Noel was so certain about us.

Why couldn't I be?

I *was* willing to try.

Maybe this was how to do it.

"I'm just so scared, Noel," I admitted as I nuzzled into him like he could save me.

Maybe he could.

Yes, keep talking.

"I've been living in fear that the other shoe will drop ever since we reunited. No, even before that I felt this way. In Sweden too. No matter where we are, Noel, I *expect* you to leave. Or to kick me out. I just can't bring myself to believe you will keep on loving me."

"But, sweetheart, I do love you," he said. "And I *will* keep on loving you."

I pulled back, crying out, "But you're too good for me. Can't you see that?"

"Maisie, stop it."

Too bad he was dealing with one stubborn soul.

"No."

I struggled to get out of his arms. But he held onto me tightly. He knew I'd run again.

He was right—that was my plan.

Noel wasn't about to let me go, not this time.

When I tried one final time to get away, I somehow ended up on my back with him sitting on top of me, my arms pinned above my head.

He believed in me so much.

He believed in us.

Why couldn't I do the same?

"You're going to listen to me," he ground out. "This bullshit ends tonight. First, it was you feeling guilty about what happened in Sweden. And now it's you fearing I'll leave."

"You will," I spat out.

"No! I told you before and I'm telling you now—I am not going anywhere! When I tell someone I love them, I mean it. I stick around."

"People say things, Noel."

That pissed him off.

"Don't take my words lightly, Maisie. All this time, you've been worried I'm the one who's going to take off. But who's the person packing a suitcase? Who is the one always running?"

"Me," I admitted.

"Yes, you."

"It's because I'm like my mother. And maybe like my dad. He left too, you know."

Noel shook his head. "You're not either of them, not deep down where it counts. You are simply you. You need to believe that."

Did I?

Could I?

I wasn't sure.

Noel went on, "Maisie, you need to realize that you're using all those things as excuses. You're afraid, but you need to be brave. Trust in us, okay?"

In a tiny voice, I confessed, "I don't really want to go."

He loosened his grip on my pinned wrists, sighing, "Then don't."

It was like it finally hit me then, harder and more intensely than anything ever before. I finally saw the truth, so damn clearly.

Life is like that, you know?

Sometimes you fight something so hard and for so long, until you suddenly realize there was never any reason to. You had made things bigger in your head, like a child who believes there are monsters in her closet.

Well, my monsters were about to get evicted.

It was a life-defining moment.

I could continue on as a scared little girl, or I could become a strong woman.

I chose strong.

Noel probably thought I was crazy when I peered up at him and said, "You really do love me, don't you?"

He dragged his hand down his chiseled face, murmuring, "You're killing me, Mais."

Softly, I said, "I do love you too much. Maybe that's what's been scaring me all along. No, I know it is. And I've been giving in to that fear. But I'm not doing it any longer."

"Are you certain you can live with your fear?" he replied. "Because I hate to break it to you, but love is almost always scary. And it rarely gets easier."

I blew out a breath. "I know. But I'm willing to try."

Lowering himself down onto me, he said, "Does that mean you're not leaving?"

"I don't think I can," I teased. "You're on top of me, pinning me down."

"Be serious, Mais."

"Okay, okay." I smiled up at him. "Yes, I'm not leaving."

"And no more freak-outs?" he hedged.

"No more freak-outs."

He narrowed his eyes at me. "How can I believe you?"

I slid my arms up around his neck and told him, "You're going to have to trust me on that one, okay?"

He blew out a breath. "I guess that we'll both have to trust each other."

"I think that about sums it up."

Shaking his head, he chuckled. "Good thing I love you, woman."

"Mmm, it is a good thing. And it's a good thing I love you too. But I'm thinking, after all this, I should probably *show* you."

I arched up, my lips meeting his.

He knew what I meant and offered no resistance, not that I thought he would.

Feeling like a new person, one who deserved every good thing she had coming to her, I got to work on showing Noel Sandlund just how much I loved and trusted him.

And I think he saw that I, Maisie Troy, was finally all in.

ALL IN

NOEL

There were no more setbacks.

Maisie told me she finally was all in with our relationship, and she was.

Maybe she had needed to break and hit rock bottom, before she could be built back up.

That's what the night of the last preseason game had been—the final crash and burn.

And now it was the rise of the phoenix.

Maisie was back to herself, and she was the best version yet.

We made so many wonderful memories over the next several weeks.

I played great hockey, and she embraced her new life. Even when her mother called from California with an update on her new life with

Gary, Maisie held up just fine.

When I asked her why talking with her mom hadn't affected her negatively, she told me the reason.

"I finally realized that it's okay to be a little part of her. And even a little bit of my dad. I'm bigger than those small parts, like you said. I'm me. And I finally like myself."

God, she was so healthy.

I loved it.

"Babe…" I picked her up and spun her around in a wide circle. "You may like yourself, but I love you so fucking much."

When I set her down, she giggled, "I love you too."

I raised a brow. "No more lingering doubts about us and our future?"

"Not a one."

She stood on her tiptoes and kissed me.

I knew then that we'd be all right.

And we were.

We finally even looked at the photo album with her dad in them. There were only a few pics of the man, he was tall and had dark hair, but I think it did Maisie good seeing him.

She'd finally learned to use the past as a catalyst to make her stronger.

By Christmas, we were closer than ever.

Since there was a short break with no games scheduled, I asked her if she'd like to take a little trip.

"Where to?" Maisie asked.

I held up the plane tickets I'd already bought, and said, "How about we go to Sweden?"

Her eyes widened. "Oh my God, Noel, I'd love to. But you don't have *that* much time off."

Yes, it'd have to be a short trip.

But that didn't matter.

I had plans.

Oh, did I have plans.

"That's true," I concurred. "But even a few days away are better than none. Besides, where's your sense of adventure?"

"Oh, you…" She gave me a playful push. "Come on. Let's go pack."

"Ah, that's the spirit."

Later that night, we were on a red-eye across the Atlantic. I'd booked first class, of course, so we could get plenty of sleep in the fold-down beds.

As a result, we arrived in Sweden feeling fairly well-rested.

I'd arranged for a limo to take us to the same hotel where we met.

After we got our luggage, we hopped in.

On the way, when I glanced over, Maisie was smiling.

She recognized the route.

"Are you happy?" I asked.

"I am," she said.

We were too.

It didn't even matter that it was snowy and cold in Stockholm. It was actually ideal. We lived in the desert, so the change was welcomed.

Once we were checked into the hotel, Maisie and I took a walk down to Old Town. Snowflakes fell all around us, blanketing the ground in white.

"Wow. Good thing I brought boots." Maisie nodded down to her feet.

I wrapped my arm around her as we walked. "Yes, good thing."

Decorations were up for the holidays, making the atmosphere

magical.

We thoroughly enjoyed our winter stroll.

By the time we returned to the hotel, dinner was waiting for us. We sat down to a delicious meal of lobster and steak.

When we were done eating, I leaned back in my chair.

"So, Maisie, what do you want to do now?"

She shrugged. "I don't know. I'm kind of up for anything."

"Good to hear." I smiled over at her. "What do you say we go up to the rooftop?"

Maisie didn't know it yet, but I planned to recreate the night I'd reserved the scenic rooftop for our first date. Since it was cold out this time around, I'd asked the hotel staff to secure a bunch of those tall patio heaters so it wouldn't be too frigid.

Maisie wasn't worried about the cold one bit, though.

She said, "Oh, Noel, I love that idea."

Jumping up, she rushed over to her suitcase, which in true Maisie fashion was lying open on the floor.

Pulling out a hat and woolen mittens, she said, "I'm ready."

Laughing, I grabbed my coat and helped her into hers.

A few minutes later, once we stepped out onto the rooftop, Maisie gasped in awe.

It was exactly the response I was hoping for. See, I'd not only secured the heaters, but I'd asked the staff to decorate.

And man, had they ever.

There were colorful twinkling lights everywhere—draped around the edges of the rooftop and wrapped around the lampposts, even trailing up the heater poles.

There was also a light snow falling.

The staff hadn't arranged that—fate had.

I took that as a sign.

The rooftop was beautiful, but not as gorgeous as Maisie. She was stunning. Even in her faux fur-lined hooded coat, her cute fuzzy mittens, and her pom-pom woolen cap, she took my breath away.

"Maisie," I said.

She turned to me, and I dropped down to one knee.

This was it!

In my hand, I held an open black velvet box. Inside rested a big diamond solitaire ring.

Eyes widening, Maisie said, "Oh, Noel…"

I'd taken her breath away, just as I'd hoped.

Her pause gave me the chance to ask the most important question in my entire life.

"Maisie, will you marry me?"

Tentatively, she touched the box.

"Yes," she whispered. "Oh my God, yes."

My smile was ear-to-ear as I slipped the ring on her finger.

I stood then, lifting her up and spinning her around.

"You've just made me the happiest person on the planet," I said.

"No, wait." She giggled as I spun her once more. "That can't be right."

I stopped. "Do tell, why's that?"

"Because *I'm* the happiest person on the planet right now, that's why."

I set her down, and then we agreed to be the happiest two people on the planet together.

And you know what?

I knew we were.

We had returned to where we'd begun. And yes, there'd been a few rough spots along the way. But it had been a journey, and I wouldn't have changed it for the world.

Not one little bit.

Because that journey had led us here—to love and happiness, and to the promise of a life spent together.

One I knew would be the very best.

No illusions, just real.

THE END

Up next in the Boys of Winter hockey romance series is Blake's story, FORBIDDEN ON ICE

And in the Men of Fall football romance series, look for Caleb's story, *Fair Catch*, to release in October 2019.

ABOUT THE AUTHOR

S.R. Grey is an Amazon Top 30 and a #1 Barnes & Noble bestselling author. Her bestselling hockey rom-com series, and new football series, feature a different hot player in every story. All of the books can be read in any order since they're interconnected standalones.

Ms. Grey's novels have appeared on multiple Amazon bestseller lists, including the Top 100 several times. She is also a Top 100 bestselling author on iTunes.

Author Website (stop on by to see how pretty it is):
http://srgrey.com/

S.R. Grey's Facebook page is a hoot:
http://www.facebook.com/SRGrey

S.R. Grey's Facebook Reading Group is even MORE fun:
https://www.facebook.com/groups/SRGreyHardAbsandHotBooks/

Sign up for S.R. Grey's newsletter (you know you want to):
http://mad.ly/signups/106801/join

S.R. Grey on Twitter (for the random tweets):
https://twitter.com/AuthorSRGrey

S.R. Grey on Instagram for the riveting pics (well, she thinks so):
http://instagram.com/authorsrgrey

S.R. Grey Goodreads Author page:
http://www.goodreads.com/author/show/6433082.S_R_Grey

Wait!

It's not over yet.

Read the first chapter of **Forward Progress**, the first novel in the bestselling *Men of Fall* series, where football meets romance.

Chapter One:
Leaving Las Vegas

Graham

I hesitate, my pen hovering over the yellow sheet of legal paper on my desk as I contemplate what to write.

What am I doing?

I'm making a list of what I'd like to achieve throughout the second half of this year. But damn, it's no easy task.

I want to get this done, though. The rehab I went through a couple of years ago made me a big believer in things like setting goals and writing out lists.

My brain is usually racing when I write these kinds of things. I have so much to get down on paper that my pen moves too fast, leaving my sentences a jumbled blur of words I have to decipher later.

Today, however, I've got nothing.

Maybe because all my most recent goals have been achieved…and therefore checked off.

Like this one—I wanted to have my own gym business *and* make it a raging success.

Check, check.

Both of those objectives have been achieved.

And then there's my ongoing goal of always trying to give back and help others.

Check that off too.

I'm still an active sponsor for Narcotics Anonymous, even if it is only for one guy these days—Las Vegas Wolves hockey player Benjamin Perry.

Still counts, though, right?

Ah, but Perry hardly needs me anymore. He's doing really well on his own.

In the past, I always had my sister, Chloe, to worry about. She wasn't in NA or anything, but she had her share of troubles in the relationship department. Seemed I was always swooping in to rescue her.

But she met and married someone great—Dylan Culderway, another hockey player I'm friends with. Chloe now has a calm and happy life. She and Dylan even have a baby on the way.

Fuck, I can't wait to be an uncle.

I spend a few minutes wondering if their baby will have dark blonde hair and cerulean blue eyes like my sister and I do, or if she'll have brown eyes and dark hair like Dylan.

Oh hell, I'm just stalling.

"Get to work on that list, Graham," I mutter to myself to conjure up some motivation. "There has to be at least *one* important thing you have yet to achieve."

And there is.

But it's the one goal I've resisted writing down, on this or any prior lists.

Maybe because this goal is the most important of all and putting it down on paper gives it life. That means it's something I'll *have* to achieve.

No excuses.

"Just write it down, dumbass," I hiss. "Do it. It's the one thing you've wanted more than anything these past three years."

What is this big goal?

It's to play professional football again.

Shit, it's out there now.

I mean, I can't unthink it.

"But what if I *can't* play like I once did?" I whisper, like that would be the worst thing in the world.

Hell, it would.

Other thoughts race through my mind…

What if my once promising football career is really and truly over?

What if I'm washed up?

Do you see now why I'm afraid to write down this goal?

"But you were good." I touch pen to paper, willing my hand to move. "No, you were fucking great, Graham Tettersaw."

It's true, I was. I had a completion percentage in the 65 percent range, and I passed for over 3000 yards every season I played.

I also averaged 30+ touchdowns a year, meaning I was rarely intercepted.

Not to mention, the fans fucking loved me.

I was a god, damn it!

But then I got hurt, and a god I was no more. I was just a man, a man with a blown knee and a crappy attitude. Hence the prescription drug addiction. I just didn't care.

The team I was playing for at the time—the Arizona Cardinals—cut my ass. Doctors, really good ones, told me I'd never play again.

Down in the dumps about, well, just about everything, I developed that nasty painkiller addiction.

That led me to NA.

It worked, and I got clean and sober.

I still am—painkiller-free for over three years now.

That's why I like to give back as a sponsor. It's the least I can do. I believe if I can overcome addiction, anyone can.

"So what would everyone you've helped want you to do now?" I ask myself out loud.

I know the answer. It's simple, really.

They'd want me to believe in myself as much as I believed in them.

That finally gets the pen moving and I write down the one goal that means the world to me—I want to play professional football again.

Shit, that feels good.

On a roll, I jot down another—I'd like to be picked up by a good team.

Problem with that is I'm thirty years old. I'll actually be thirty-one this September, which is only four months away.

There's not much call for a quarterback in his early thirties, especially if he's been out of the game for a few years.

But I have a few things going for me…

I've kept myself in great shape. And I just landed a slick new agent.

I made that move after I discovered the one I had the past few years wasn't even trying anymore.

This new one, Jock Sosarelli, is fantastic. He represents a ton of sports figures, including some of my hockey pals. Brent Oliver is one of his clients. He's the biggest star for the Las Vegas Wolves, so that's something right there.

Jock is good, really good.

A middle-aged former professional athlete, the guy knows sports. Jock used to play baseball, like a hundred years ago.

Okay, not that long ago, but I like to tell him that.

Good thing he takes it well.

Another reason why Jock is a good fit for me is because an injury ended his career too. He understands the perils I face. That's probably why he was quick to pick me up as a new client. I think he'd like to see me get the second chance he never did.

My cell phone rings, breaking me from my reverie. And wouldn't you know it, it's Jock. He wants to FaceTime, so this must be good news.

Leaning back in the chair in my office, I hold the phone up.

Jock's silver-streaked black hair and smiling mug fill the screen.

"Hey, what's up?" I say.

"A lot," he replies. "And you're going to love this news, Tettersaw."

"Hmm…" I'm curious, but first I feel compelled to remind him, "You can call me Graham, you know?"

"Eh, sure, whatever you say, Tettersaw."

I chuckle.

So much for that.

Last names are Jock's shtick. Though I've noticed when shit gets real, he uses first names.

"Okay, so what's this great news, Jock?"

Sliding his reading glasses up the bridge of his nose, he peers down at what looks like a contract of some sort. I've seen enough, I should know.

My heart starts beating like crazy. *Could this be a football deal?* I want this so badly.

As my excitement builds, he says, "I think I have something in the works for you."

I have a shot at making a team? I need to know, but I'm afraid to ask.

But I must.

So, slowly, I murmur, "What kind of something are we talking about here?"

Without looking up from what just has to be a contract, Jock says, "There's a team expressing great interest in you, Graham."

Whoa, he just used my first name. This is the real deal. And that is definitely a contract in his hands.

Fuck.

He goes on, "This team would like to fly you out to their mini-camp. It's going on right now. You could run some reps so they can see you in action, verify your arm is still strong—"

"It is," I interrupt.

Jock talks right over me. "—*and* to make certain your knee is no longer a problem."

I assure him my knee's not an issue at all, and he says, "Good. We'll have to move fast then, if you're interested."

Am I interested?

Is he crazy?

Laughing, I assure him, "I'm interested, Jock. Fuck, trust me, I am."

"Good to hear. If this team likes what they see"—he picks up the contract and waves it in the air, making the screen blur—"they're prepared to follow through on a more-than-fair offer."

My breath catches in my throat. Could this be the shot I've been wishing and hoping for? Hell, the ink's not even dry on my list of new goals.

This is almost too good to be true, though.

So, erring on the side of caution, I inquire, "Which team are we talking about here, Jock?"

He replies "the Columbus Comets," and my heart sinks.

I knew this was too perfect.

"Did you say the Comets?" I verify.

"Yes, the new team in Columbus, Ohio."

I blow out a disappointed breath. "I know who you mean. They're part of the new football league. The one created just last year."

"Yes, that's them," Jock confirms.

"They're not the NFL, Jock."

Instantly, he snaps, "No, Tettersaw, they're not. But we're still talking about a damn fine opportunity."

He's not entirely wrong.

I'm just torn.

Last year, a two-country league emerged. Comprised of twenty-six teams in the US and Canada, this start-up organization managed to cobble together a surprisingly successful inaugural season.

So, yeah, it's not all bad.

"You're right, Jock," I concede, sighing. "But just so you know, the Comets are *not* my first choice by any means."

He chuckles. "I'm sure they're not, Graham. But there's a lot of chatter that this new league is the league of the future. Think about it for a minute. We're talking fan bases in *two* countries. There's so much room for expansion. This is a good opportunity, my man. And the terms the Comets have outlined for you, if you were to be picked up, are more than equitable."

"Ah, hell,"—I run my hand down my face—"I just don't know."

Blowing out a clearly frustrated breath, Jock says, "I'm going to lay it on the line for you. You're not getting any younger, Tettersaw. That means you can pretty much forget about making a comeback in the NFL. The way that league see things, you had your chance. Now you're just a washed-up former star who carries around a history of painkiller problems."

"Hey!" I bristle. "I only had that problem once. And it was ages ago. I've come a long way since then."

Jock is unruffled, no surprise there.

"Hey, hey, don't get pissed at me. I'm just telling you the way it is. You want a chance to start as a quarterback at the professional level?"

"Yes, of course I do," I snap.

"Well, then this is it, my man. To be honest, this could be an opportunity for you to really shine."

"Ha-ha." I chuckle. "You mean like a comet?"

Jock laughs.

He likes that.

"Yes, I guess you could say that," he says.

"Hell, what the fuck do I have to lose?" I say. "Tell the Comets I'm interested, okay?"

"You got it. And for the record, you're making the right decision, Graham."

"I hope so," I mumble.

He ignores me and goes on. "I'll fax you the contract in a few minutes. You can look it over thoroughly. I'll also book you a flight to Columbus."

"Perfect, thanks."

After we wrap up, I place my cell on the desk. And then I think about what this means.

Following some serious contemplation, I begin to feel pretty good about this opportunity. I mean, hell, everything Jock said to me is true. The Columbus Comets may not be part of the NFL, but they're no chumps. And, more importantly, they're offering me a chance to play professional football again.

So Columbus, Ohio, hmm…

That's a long way from Las Vegas, where I currently live. But this could be the push I've needed to start a life of my own.

I'm not talking football anymore. No. These past few years I've spent so much time helping others that I've kind of neglected my own self. Even my sister tells me that.

And it's true. I have no wife, no girlfriend, no kids, and, outside of the gym business, no real life.

Shit.

Picking up the pen, I add one more goal to my list—*leave Las Vegas and start a new life.*

Yeah, I like that one.

Because, just like in football, in order to win, you have to have forward progress.

Continue reading *Forward Progress*:
https://amzn.to/2s4zM3W